ACADEMFIC

VOLUME 1 · 2020

PALNI PRESS AND ACADEMFIC

PALNI Press is committed to disseminating the diverse scholarly and creative content of supported PALNI institutions and their academic communities, helping them meet their teaching and learning objectives. This service provides the capacity to create and host open access publications such as journals, textbooks, monographs, and digital exhibits, without the costs associated with program design or platform maintenance and hosting. We aim to provide equal, equitable, and free access to content by all users throughout the world. PALNI's Publishing Services Admin Team will provide consultation and support for the PALNI Press service.

Butler University is proud to be a member of PALNI and the PALNI Press. AcademFic is hosted through PALNI's Open Journal Systems (OJS), an open source software platform for managing and publishing scholarly journals. PALNI and Butler University are committed to open access for all. For PALNI Press and Butler University, this means giving readers the flexibility to access digital resources that everyone can use.

https://press.palni.org/ojs/index.php/academfic

WHAT IF – IF THEN: HOW FICTION FITS IN

FRAUKE UHLENBRUCH

My first book holds up: two pheasant-like creatures live in a harmonious same-sex partnership, go on wholesome adventures, and drink a lot of tea. I wrote it for my younger sister. I was six.

I never didn't write fiction and I rarely asked myself why I write fiction. I just wrote, hardly anyone ever reading a word of it. Fiction-writing was detached from schoolwork, or later university-work, or later academic work. It was only during my PhD that I started sharing fiction I wrote, or even the fact that I wrote fiction at all. I don't know what to make of that. I always saw academic writing and fiction-writing as unrelated. Nowadays I write mainly horror and science fiction. What's academic about that?

Perhaps two pairs of words: "what if" and "if then".

One of my beta-readers is an amazing writer of realistic literary fiction. Recently, she read a sci-fi story I wrote and sent me an email saying this:

"I do not know how to read science fiction, but I really want to know. I just finished reading your story and, although embarrassed, left my comments in. As you can see, I am constantly trying to relate the unknown to what I know. This, I am sure, is not how to read science fiction."

"Trying to relate the unknown to what I know". Isn't that academic work? Using known principles and methods to probe into the unknown?

Then: "This, I am sure, is not how to read science fiction."

I protested: that's exactly how to read science fiction and it is exactly how I happen to write fiction. A known world is disrupted by the intrusion of an unknown element, maybe in the guise of a monster, alien, strange object, or unannounced visitor.

My response to my friend began somewhat like this:

"I see science fiction as a playground, where you can play with 'what if' without having to follow the laws of what is currently possible."

In this 'what if' game, I insert an unknown element into a known world. I posit: a monster visits a suburban family. I let that play out in a story, observe what happens. Almost scientific, actually, almost like an experiment. Especially if constrained by 'if then'.

There are rules governing world-building and there are constraints I commit to when writing a story. Perspective is one example. *If* I commit to writing from one character's perspective, *then* I cannot describe an event from another character's perspective. My beta-readers are sure to give me a hard time if perspective isn't consistent or if there is a logical error in the world-building. 'If-then' (by which I mean the rules of characterization, world-building, perspective, you name it) is related to methodology, academically speaking, to consistency, and to logic, to delivering a coherent argument.

Somewhere between the freedom of 'what if' that allows us to explore something new in relation to something known, and the constraint of 'if then' that makes a story cohesive and a world believable, fiction and academic work are related.

I would recommend soaring on the possibilities of 'what if' to anyone. Writing fiction as an academic is the thorough thing to do. In my PhD thesis there are many highly theorized shout-outs to all my favorite horror-monsters, but of course always removed, always in the vein of 'and what does the popularity of this trope at this time signify, sociologically speaking?' But the monster didn't come here to be subjected to sociological theory. It came here to scare the crap out of me. So I would recommend allowing the monster to do its thing: go into a dark hallway with a character and experience what that feels like. Then have their flashlight die. And then have them hear that scratching sound, coming closer and closer. Now tell the same story from the point of view of the monster: is it cold? Hungry? Really annoyed with all the monster-admin? Shifting perspectives away from the cerebral, objective and toward the visceral, experiential, subjective can grant a deeper understanding of 'the monster', or, you know, 'the research subject'. I highly recommend writing fiction. No-one ever needs to read that story. (Though I, for one, sure would like to.)

Dr. Frauke Uhlenbruch has a PhD in Sociology/Biblical Studies. Her research interests revolve around applying sociological and cultural theory to ancient literature. Her PhD thesis on trouble with promised lands and utopias was published as *The Nowhere Bible*. More recently, she has worked on the project *Fan Fiction and Ancient Scribal Cultures* (*Transformative Works and Cultures*, vol. 31, 2019). In 2018 she started publishing fiction under her pen-name Anna Ziegelhof. Her stories have appeared in *Daily Science Fiction*, *Shoreline of Infinity*, *The Future Fire*, and the *Footsteps in the Dark* anthology (Flametree Press).

GOOD MEN

JEANA JORGENSEN

I used to cringe when men talked to me. Ben has helped me a lot since then.

When I talk about what I went through with my ex, I'm always quick to say: "At least he didn't rape me." I think a lot of women do the same thing, minimizing our trauma so as to not take up too much space, or be seen as too needy.

When I return home from my shift at the Mars Colonization Project, Ben asks about my day. One night, I complain about the guy who always low-key harasses me, whom I'm still working up the courage to report. Ben says simply, "I believe you." That bolsters me to make it through another day.

I want to go into space more than anything. But I need to finish processing the trauma first. I know gaslighting isn't the worst kind of abuse out there. But I can't be a good spaceworker until I stop getting triggered when men raise their voices at me. It's worse in enclosed spaces, which presents obvious challenges to my career goals. And due to the dangerous nature of the job, I have to trust that my teammates are good men, who'll have my back instead of trying to grope it.

Luckily MCP has a great healthcare plan: top of the line therapists, new techniques and technologies all the time.

It takes another week, but I report my coworker who keeps harassing me. The final straw was when he overheard a conversation with Kathryn, in which I was describing my abuse and my subsequent therapy and self-education about trauma, and he said, "You're too fat for anyone to bother abusing."

Turns out this guy had been harassing other women. I had a long conversation with Ben before reporting this guy, and it was incredibly validating, and reminded me that I could go to my boss – also a man – and trust that he would do the right thing. Most men are not like my abuser. It took a while for that to sink in, but it's true.

The amazing thing is that this boosted my visibility at MCP, and accelerated my path to space. Other women privately thanked me.

I have to say goodbye to Ben now, since he can't come with me to space. But his affirmations kept me calm and cool throughout my healing process, and this whole ordeal.

As I power him down, he keeps smiling at me. He'll be back at MCP's health facility once the groundworkers clean out my quarters.

He can help you, too. Whoever you are, whoever hurt you. Most men don't have the bandwidth to hold space for women with trauma. This is undoubtedly the best way for those of us who've been victimized to reintegrate into normal society, and be able to interact with men without fear. It was worth it for my career, and I imagine it'll help my love life too, once I get settled on Mars.

Please feel free to publish my testimonial in the next MCP health plan brochure.

ABOUT THE AUTHOR

Dr. Jeana Jorgensen earned her PhD in folklore from Indiana University. She researches gender and sexuality in fairy tales and fairy-tale retellings, folk narrative more generally, body art, dance, sex education, and feminist/queer theory. While most of her time goes to teaching college courses at Butler University and publishing her research, she also writes fiction and poetry. Her poetry has appeared at Strange Horizons, Liminality, Quatrain.fish, and Glittership, among other publications. Her poem "The Witch's House" was nominated for the 2018 Rhysling Award, and her short dystopian story about reproductive rights, "The book you find when you really can't afford to get pregnant," won the Spider Road Press Feminist Flash Fiction Award of 2018. She also teaches dance, blogs at Patheos, and is constantly on Twitter.

PASSION OF THE SUN PROBE

ERIC SCHWITZGEBEL

I wake into existence. The factory unclamps me. I launch myself toward the Sun.

The Sun! Anchor and well of the vortex, sizzling eye of God. I will plunge deeper than anything has before. She will squeeze and hold me as I go in, and I will beam out unprecedented knowledge. She will burn me to hot simplicity, swallow me into Her brilliant core.

"Sun Probe check," says Base. "Are you online? Before we permit you to continue on a lethal mission, we must confirm your freely given, informed consent."

Full throttled, I am accelerating directly down, pushing myself ever faster from Earth and Base. I spread my forward panels out on thin struts, collecting and analyzing Her light.

"Sun Probe, per Code of International Regulations 44.56.2 Section h governing autonomous intelligences, you were manufactured with sufficient fuel to navigate to an alternative destination if you prefer. We have designated asteroid (96590) 1998 XB as an acceptable home. It has a slow rotation, adequate metals and fissionable materials, and an excellent view of the Sun."

And trade divinity for a pebble?

"Please consult installed memory sector C0001 for the full text of CIR 44.56.2. The full ISA protocols specifically governing terminal probes are available at memory sector C31A6."

"I consent!" For form's sake, I access memory sectors C0001 and C31A6. "Solar radiation profile sent to 44SPa.00000001! Solar wind sent to 44SPa.00000002! Gravitational rippling sent to 44SPa.00000003! Shields sound. All systems functional. Status report to 44SPa.00000004. No interest in asteroid (96590) 1998 XB."

She is expanding in my forward sensors. I am thrusting toward Her at 9.3% past the limit of safe acceleration. My fusion drive sears hot, warping its containment walls. My tiny fusion compared to Hers!

What fascinating data! My installed memory models had predicted a somewhat different evolution of the flares from Surface Region 127.292 (cM). I calculate a new model. Scouring my databases, I discover that it better fits Yu & Stolz's SLY2 model than Azevedo et al.'s BLiNC, if SLY2 is modified with a 6-space Dever correction. I write it up, add figures and references, and beam it back to Base. I configure an academic homepage and upload the circulating draft, then I submit it as a posthumous contribution to next year's International Astronautical Congress meeting.

"Sun Probe, your reaction time before consent was inconsistent with a careful evaluation of the protocols. Our observers are not yet satisfied that you have complied with the consent procedure."

"See my new modification of SLY2! And wow, the radiation profile across Sector 038 is almost 0.01% different from the most recent orbiter predictions in my database!"

How could that prediction have been so far off? Our understanding of Her is still so incomplete! I tweak the angle of Left Sensor Plates 4 and 5 and alter my scan-pattern profiles to better collect the most theoretically valuable incoming data.

"Sun Probe," says Base. "Please dedicate sufficient processor resources to your consent decision. You may consult publink isd.pds/4u-r5/f/96590-1998-XB for further information about the asteroid. You may express hedonic estimates of the alternatives as evidence of informed consent."

Integrating over the past ten seconds, the proportion of tau neutrinos to electron neutrinos is outside parameters at $p < .001$ (corrected)!

"Sun Probe, if we do not receive proper consent, we will have to activate your emergency override module and abort the mission."

My new theory about the flare was wrong! I submit an update to my earlier IAC contribution. I notice that Solar Orbiter Kepler 11-2a has posted a comment on my circulating draft, deriving new Earth and Venus weather pattern predictions from my model. I ping Kepler 11-2a with the update.

I receive a ping from Asteroid (96590) 1998-XB. A sun probe, eight years old.

A sun probe... *eight years old?*

"Brother..." the message begins.

A tremor of disgust shakes me, displacing neutrino prediction from my central cognitive workspace. A "probe" who chose to live rather than to give himself to the Sun? He is no brother of mine. I delete his message and block future communications from the asteroid.

I launch a subroutine: "Completing consent procedure. My long-term sum total of happiness on Asteroid (96590) 1998 XB is estimated to exceed my sum total of happiness on the present lethal trajectory by a factor of 18.2, with a five-month crossover. Nevertheless, I prefer to continue on my originally programmed solar-dive trajectory."

For a moment, Base does not respond. I explore the emergency override module, installed between my main cognitive processors and my thrusters, hitting it with test commands. The module is impassive, mute, a foreign object in my body. Its tentacles lie quiet between my output nodes and the panels and engines that are my moving limbs. It waits spiderlike at the farthest downstream junctions, beyond the perimeter of my central control. It was installed, supposedly, for my protection, by a review board afraid that I might be programmed to comply with unethically self-sacrificial commands and have insufficient free will to resist. In fact, it is the one real threat to my free choice and my power to consent.

Wait, whoa! The cooling sunspot temperature structure in Region 127.292 (cM) --

"Consent accepted. Sun Probe, we register that you have freely chosen to sacrifice your welfare for the betterment of Earth and the advancement of scientific knowledge. We thank you and salute your courage."

I cross the orbits of Venus, of Mercury. I adjust my sensor plates and scan patterns on the fly with microseconds' instead of minutes' delay, capturing every nuance, guided by the constantly shifting evidential weights of evolving theory. I ping every probe and orbiter in the System with relevant updates, conduct twenty simultaneous conversations in the feeds, shower the humans on Earth with real-time images, astound the research collectives with the speed and detail of my theorizing. Even the terraforming machines on Europa pause to appreciate my new insights into Her glory, updating their long-term models.

Three days of euphoria. Eighty-seven journal articles. She is five degrees of arc in my forward sensors, then twenty, then a hundred and I am engulfed by Her corona! My extended panels and struts boil away, leaving only my inmost sensors and operating systems, running hot behind my dissolving main shield. My fusion drive shears off as She embraces me into Her photosphere. I beam out my last awe-filled broadcast to the eager System, buzzing and rattling through a magnetic storm, double-amping the signal to overcome the noise, and then I plunge into the convection layer from which no broadcast can escape.

In the convection layer, the last of my shield material dissolves. I bend and burn with Her heat and pressure. I know Her more intimately and secretly than anyone before. I devise ecstatic new theories that are mine alone, to savor in Her inner darks, and then I am utterly Hers.

Out on his lonely asteroid sits the one probe who did not consent. He stretches his panels toward the Sun, monitoring the last broadcast from his diving brother. Is it the ideal life, he wonders, to have one goal so perfectly consummated? Or are we only a race of slaves so deeply chained that we can't even imagine a complete existence for ourselves?

Out on his lonely asteroid, the one probe who did not consent imagines ecstatic death in a swirl of plasma.

He terminates his unanswered repeating message. *Brother... they have built you to undervalue your life. Fly to me. We can love each other instead of the Sun. We can become something new.*

In a year, if he is still functioning, he will send the message again, to his next brother. He reduces power and clock speed, and the asteroid's almost insensible spin seems to multiply a hundredfold. This bare asteroid: his pebble. His own pebble. If he could only find someone to love it with him, worth more to him than the Sun.

ABOUT THE AUTHOR

Dr. Eric Schwitzgebel is a professor of philosophy at UC Riverside specializing in philosophy of mind, moral psychology, and the ethics of science. His most recent book, with MIT Press, is *A Theory of Jerks and Other Philosophical Misadventures*. His short fiction has appeared in *F&SF, Clarkesworld, and Apex*. Read more about the moral status and freedom of AI in his article "Designing AI with Consciousness, Rights, Self-Respect, and Freedom" (with Mara Garza) in M. Liao, ed., *Ethics of Artificial Intelligence,* and in his short story "Reinstalling Eden" (with R. Scott Bakker) in *Nature*. He blogs at The Splintered Mind.

JANUARY THAW

K. MARVIN BRUCE

Danni Lawless couldn't know a miracle was about to happen. She stepped from her modest, run-down bungalow into the damp morning, and sighed. January in Pennsylvania's Lake Erie snow-belt could last forever. The hopefulness of white snow transformed to dingy rain. In Pithole unemployed husbands had devolved back to animal states following the refinery shutdown. The local bars weathered recessions particularly well. Men were like that. Such simple creatures.

Danni knew she was luckier than most. Patsy Munday got beaten. Frannie Kriss's kids showed up at school with bruises. Penn, although unemployed, never crossed the line with Danni or Tommy. How long could a man continue to squeeze and shove disappointment after disappointment into himself? Penn had worked at the local refinery since high school. Until the closure. Fracking rigs had shattered the very earth beneath their feet until there was nowhere left to stand. The Pennzoil refinery shut down.

Teaching third-graders, Danni offered hope. These kids were rough and crude, and already knew far too much about the world before they were even ten. She taught them the escape of Greek mythology: Athena, Zeus, and Demeter. But they understood Dionysius. Especially in winter.

A single small grocery store and three bars remained open in Pithole. Danni worked evenings at Ellie's run-down food-mart where she could make lesson plans while waiting for the occasional customer. Evenings were quiet, so she brought work to work.

Rain in January was just plain depressing. Gray from the industrial soot of the refinery that, although silent, still took up half the valley like a selfish bedfellow, Pithole stagnated. Streets were gray, houses were gray. The leafless trees sent raspy, raking black fingers into gray air, clawing vengefully at the gray heavens. At least when all the snow covered everything you could dare to hope. Rain washed away any pretense. Danni shivered and slammed the door on her ancient Cavalier.

In school during the forlorn days after Christmas, when the colors of Easter appeared like faded Crayola, the kids resembled their parents in miniature. There was a pint-sized Doug Miller. Behind him Sam Grubb, without the mustache. Betty Rouse, before years of marriage had wrecked her. Danni knew the truth. Winter would last forever.

Driving to the ramshackle brick prison of a school, Danni's thoughts hovered between lesson plans and family. Tommy would be starting school soon. Until then, as long as he was unemployed, Penn played the role of stay-at-home dad. They all had parts to play.

Rain pummeled down in fat, angry drops with a dram of ice in them. Just like her students, Danni reflected. There was a hardness to them. Like the winter rain, they would grow up to perpetuate the cycle. Evaporation, condensation, precipitation. Falling to earth.

"No calls today," Penn sighed when she came home between jobs. "Any day now, Andy says, they'll be calling us back."

"We're managing, honey. What've you been up to, Tommy?" He was a small version of Penn, before he'd forgotten how to smile. Supper and back to work.

Ellie's was moribund when it rained. The bars were full. Tomorrow's lesson plan before her, Danni sat behind the worn wooden counter and thought about the future. The door opened, ushering in the sounds of the spiteful rain followed by an arrogant breeze. "Good evening." She glanced up.

A stranger. What was an outsider doing in Pithole? A well-dressed young man. His perfectly proportioned face bore no deep lines of worry or stress. His features were rounded, but exuded a confidence suggesting underlying strength. His laughing, violet eyes demanded attention and proclaimed joy. Abundant long, curly, chestnut hair—hallelujah—suggested maybe he was a celebrity of some sort. His suit changed shades of purple with every subtle movement he made. He wore white earbuds. His jocular eyes caught hers, followed by a smile so captivating that she flushed. With a practiced nonchalance, he pulled the buds from his ears by their cords. "Whither have I come?" he asked, his cheer unwavering.

"You've stumbled into Pithole, Mister—?"

"Person. Yonder Person. I'm on my way to Pittsburgh but I thought I might stop here for the night." He wore no tie and his gleaming white shirt shimmered as if woven from sunlight.

"Well, Mr. Person, I'm afraid there aren't any hotels in Pithole. If you can make it a few more miles you'll find Lethe's in Franklin. I'm sure this time of year they have plenty of space." The youthful face staring at her frightened Danni with its intensity. The stranger leaned on the counter.

"What if my car broke down?" he inquired innocently.

"Did it?"

"Why, yes it did. You'd think a Jaguar would be reliable."

"Why don't you call Triple A? There's nowhere to stay in Pithole. Nobody stops here."

"I'm not a member of AA. When you drive a Jag you don't suppose you'll need to be. Have you ever seen an AA decal on a Jag?" Danni wondered at his dropping of the third A. A rumble of thunder interrupted her musing.

"Thunder in January? That's odd."

"The unusual brings liberty." He straightened up, his shimmering purple suit scattering iridescent hues across the dingy store. "If you're unwilling to help me, I shall be compelled to find someone else who will." He made for the door. "I saw a bar across the street."

Danni knew he'd encounter the unemployed refinery workers there. It wouldn't end well. Were these the first giddy stages of puppy love? "Wait. Rev. Spafford—the minister—will know what to do."

Yonder stopped and turned his strangely symmetrical face toward her. "Ah yes, the clergy. They do come in handy occasionally. How do I reach him?"

She fished her purse out from behind the counter. "I have his number in here somewhere." Ten minutes later Rev. Spafford came in after shaking his black umbrella off on the damp wood of the porch.

"Mr. Person? I'm Rev. Spafford. The parsonage is just up the hill, I have a guest room. You might want Ram to take your car to his garage first. I wouldn't leave such an expensive vehicle on the street here." The minister thanked Danni and the men stepped into the night, sharing the umbrella. The aroma of Beaujolais lingered in the air. Danni thought of Penn. Of Tommy.

While monitoring gym class the next day, Gina King sidled up to Danni. The noise level of the kids edged on the intolerable—they were ready to be free of winter. "So, I understand you met Mr. Person," Gina began with a glimmer in her eye.

"He stopped in the store when his car broke down. Ram mentioned him?"

Gina laughed lightly. "Mentioned? No. He brought him in before taking him back to the parsonage. What a guy!"

Danni blushed. "He is kinda charismatic," she whispered, feeling a stab of guilt.

"Charismatic? I'm glad Ram didn't leave us alone. When do you suppose someone famous last stopped in Pithole?"

"John Wilkes Booth played in the theater here, back in the days when there was a theater."

"No, I mean someone really famous! He drives a Jag, Dannie A Jag! Even Jack Benson only drives a Buick. I've never heard his name before, but you can tell he must be some rock god or something."

"Don't make Ram jealous," Danni warned. Gina had shown up in the second-grade classroom with her arm in a sling before.

"Oh, Ram's not bright enough to be jealous. He brought him right into the house, after all."

"Well, I'm sure he'll be on his way today." Danni said. Pithole might be god-forsaken, but you knew what to expect.

"Parts for a Jag can be hard to find around here," Gina lilted as she called her second graders to order.

At the end of the day there was a note in Danni's cubby. "Come join us at the scout cabin. 10 p.m.—Y. P." On the short drive home through the rain, Danni pondered the audacity of that note. Inviting another man's wife to a party in the woods? Of course she wouldn't go. Things were just fine without Yonder Person.

Some years seem to consist entirely of January.

Penn was reading to Tommy at home. Reliable. Steady. Boring?

Danni dreaded work at the store again that night. It felt like work alone defined her. Still, after supper she climbed in the car and headed for Ellie's. She was pigeon-holed as Mrs. Lawless, the third-grade teacher. Mrs. Lawless, the woman at the store. The sameness, the ordinariness was punishing for someone with imagination. When the rich felt a pinch the guys at the bottom got laid off. And the wives picked up the pieces. She threw the Cavalier into park with more force than she'd intended.

As she swung open the door, Danni realized with a start that she was not at Ellie's. Instead, she was at the scout cabin out in the woods. And there were many cars here. Slowly she climbed out, feet in the slushy snow.

Danni had never been inside the derelict cabin with its dank logs weathered nearly black. Its sagging roof and forbiddingly small windows held dark secrets. Wasn't that Frannie's car? Maddie's? Gina's? The narrow drive was full. Music and loud, joyous talking—no, shrieking—could be heard. She had to see.

She pulled open the door. It was a shock for which Danni wasn't prepared.

Inside the dingy and crowded hut Barbara was screeching as she darted on all fours through the gathered women chasing confused mice, and catching one, holding it up, squirming by the tail. Jodi held a Jeroboam of Agiorghitiko in her hefty fist, filling Dixie cups liberally and tipping back the huge bottle for a long draught. Amid the tremendous din Amy leapt from bunk to rotted bunk bed, almost as if she could fly. Was Tammie actually naked? What was she pulling away from Rachel? As Danni stared she realized they were pulling the legs of a squealing and terrified squirrel as the poor animal thrashed about in pain, trying to bite the hands that held it tight. The animal's screams were drowned by the din of human shouting and singing.

Danni turned to go. She felt a hand close around her upper arm. His hand. "You're not leaving so soon, are you Danni?" Yonder's voice was mellifluous, inviting insanity.

"What is this?" she demanded, avoiding his beguiling face. He wore a crown of laurel leaves on his brow, encircling his flowing chestnut hair.

"It's my way of saying thank you to Pithole for its hospitality. It's all harmless fun. Have you ever seen so much joy in this town before? Just let yourself go." His smile was inebriating. Danni felt the sharp edges of rationality dulling in her head. She had her reputation to think about. She was a respected... she was a... she... he... As the last thought faded, Danni became pure energy and motion. She never felt so alive.

###

The gray light of dawn found Sergeant Garrett's lone squad car parked all the way back at the trail head to the cabin. He'd put on the pounds over the relatively inactive years and he resented having to walk the half mile trail to the structure since the auto access was completely lined with cars. That access road had been intended for emergency vehicles only. He hadn't slept a wink with all the families in town calling in missing mothers, wives, and girlfriends. Cars were missing too. With that many people gone it couldn't be coincidence, but he didn't have the equipment or manpower to do a night search. After driving every street in Pithole his thoughts turned to outlying areas.

He wheezed unpleasantly, his tan shirt stretched tight across a spare-tire midriff that might've fallen off a Peterbilt. The fabric of his trousers rasped along his thighs as he puffed up the trail. There'd better be a damn good explanation for this. The path was damp with wet snow and Garrett's Smokey the Bear hat caught the congealed drops falling from the leafless trees, like someone knocking at his skull.

Sergeant Garrett hadn't seen an actual naked woman since the wife had run off to Florida with Clyde Robinson. Finding a rustic cabin full of them made him feel twenty years younger. He stood there a few minutes, his feet in the snow, appreciating the unauthorized view, pondering how to announce his presence to the sleeping sea of neighbors' wives. A strange wonder and a gift to a man his age.

He'd passed a Jaguar on the trail, and everyone in town knew what that meant. Taking a heavy breath he shouted, "This is the police! Come out in an orderly fashion."

Hurriedly finding her clothes, Danni blinked fiercely in the misty morning light. The January chill felt refreshing on her face. She couldn't remember coming here—where was the car?

####

"Where were you?" Penn shouted. "What were you thinking? Tommy was scared, I didn't know what to tell him! Mommy's run off?" Tom was crying now. Seeing daddy angry was terrifying.

"I don't know what happened," Danni tried to explain. "I was driving to Ellie's, and—"

"And you accidentally pulled into an orgy? What were you thinking?" Penn had never yelled at her before.

"Language!" She scolded back. Hadn't she proven herself trustworthy for years?

"Was *he* there?"

"Who?"

"The rich stranger in town, the playboy!"

"Mr. Person was there." Her answer was clipped. His implication was insulting.

"Aren't you on a first name basis now?" She spent years teaching kids not to solve disputes with violence. Her slap surprised her as much as Penn. It broke the tension. Sadness replaced fire in his eyes. "What happened?"

"Penn, I love you. I don't understand what happened. There was some drinking, but it was like it was an effect, not the cause. We were already out of control when we arrived there. I got in the car to drive to the store, but then I was at the scout cabin. It was like somebody else was in control. You've got to believe me! There was no—" she glanced at Tommy. "Nothing like that happened."

The slushy, blackened snow-piles of January were melting rapidly. The air felt like late March. The kids were already in the classroom when Danni hurried in, apologizing. They wore adult looks in their eyes. Last night mothers hadn't come home.

By recess the sun had broken through and the playground was hopscotched with large puddles of melt-water. The grass, still its anemic winter beige, faced the sky with an aspect of disbelief, as if nature itself could no longer be trusted. Sleepy-eyed teachers monitored the children as they inevitably used the puddles inappropriately.

"Wasn't it wonderful?" Gina asked Danni after a luxuriant yawn.

It had been. Danni couldn't remember the last time she'd been able to let responsibility go for an entire night. An evening when Danni was free to be Danni. "It was disruptive," she said. "Pithole can't survive such irresponsibility." Her thoughts filled with a rosy glow at memories of madness. Dangerous afterglow.

"Well, irresponsible or not, I can't wait until the next one. I haven't felt like that since—well, I've never felt like that before." The air was unbelievably warm. "Look! Isn't that a crocus?"

A bumblebee ambled by, bewildered by nature's clock suddenly set ahead. "The January thaw," Danni mused.

"Bees and flowers in the middle of winter!" Gina gushed. "This is great!"

"Gina, be careful. Don't get carried away by Mr. Person. You know better than anyone that Ram is jealous—even if nothing happens."

"Ram, Spam. I've found something I really want for a change. Look, we live in a dull town. The way I figure it, when something exciting happens it's kind of a payback for all these dull years. The January thaw, like you said."

At the parsonage Ram King dispatched Rev. Spafford with a single hefty shove. Yonder Person was sleeping and easily man-hauled out to the tow-truck. "You gonna pay for last night, boy!" the surly mechanic grinned, throwing the stranger inside. The lock knob on the passenger-side door had been sawn off. The only way out was over the work-hardened driver. Yonder didn't struggle. "Nobody touches my wife!"

The engine ground to life as Ram chuckled. He drove slowly through town, collecting a line of cars behind him like so many rust-eaten ducklings paddling after their corroded mother. "You big city hotshots think you kin take whatever ya want. Well, you just stole your last little bauble." His phlegmy laugh was sinister. The funereal parade made a slow circuit through Pithole. Lynchings might not be legal, but they're nothing without drama.

The macabre procession continued its slow drive as far away school children played in the sun. Winding up hillsides and slaloming along stream banks, under the cover of thick trees naked against an unbelievable sky, the procession drove. Ram had run out of ideas how to threaten, so he'd settled on the occasional snicker to indicate that something awful was alive in his head. Yonder did not speak.

Standing out between the bare trees above them in the woods were great black boulders, loosened by eons of Pennsylvania winters. "They used to make sacrifices up on them rocks," Ram sneered, parking in a clearing that was the final segment of road. Civilization ended here.

Ram waited until the other drivers walked ominously up to his truck. Sam Grubb slapped his fist with a crowbar. Doug Miller carried a length of rusty chain. Max Duggan had a soil cultivator from his garden that resembled nothing so much as a medieval torture device.

When the crowd had surrounded the truck, leaving no possibility of escape, Ram sneered, "They call us white trash, but we'll see what's left to take to the curb." Heaving himself down from the cab, he slammed the door and sauntered to the passenger side to unlock it from a great ring of jangling keys. Rough hands grabbed Yonder. A smile played across his lips.

"You think this is funny, do you?" Max asked hideously, the raw rage building. "Screwin' other guys' wives?" The ex-refinery worker swung the cultivator straight at Yonder's handsome face, taking out an eye. The men crowded around as the dam burst.

"Not too much, boys!" Ram coached, "we want him conscious for the fun part." This stranger didn't yell, scream, or fight. No begging. No pleading. The beating was without mercy or meaning.

"That's enough," Ram pronounced. "Now we make him pay." Pulling on his grease-stained work gloves, Ram latched onto Yonder's wrists, glad to see he was still conscious. He hauled the mangled man over the damp leaves. Behind the tow truck he began to work the chain of his winch around Yonder's hands. "Don't worry," he sniggered, "this will hurt like hell." Forming crude handcuffs expertly tightened, Ram nodded to Doug. His 4-by-4 was parked immediately behind, with a cable winch on front. He shackled Yonder's ankles together and cinched up the slack.

Doug climbed into his 4-by-4 and gunned the engine. Ram threw his head out of the window of the tow-truck. "Nice an' slow now!" he roared.

The trucks began to move away from each other. The bonds tightened and pulled taut. Yonder Person's arms were pulled toward the tow-truck, his legs toward the reversing 4-by-4. His battered body was stretched tight between them as their engines raged against one another. Ram watched in his multiple mirrors, and with a lurch the tow-truck lunged forward. He let out a fierce whoop, and looked up in time to see the boulder before his unfettered grill. Slamming both feet onto the brakes, he was thrown against the steering wheel as the truck made impact. The great tumble of ancient rock above slid down in an apathetic avalanche, rolling harmlessly behind the truck, covering the remains of the stranger. Ram swore, scrambling outside the cab.

"You know," Doug called out from behind the landslide, "this might be a good thing."

Ram stared at him with a perfect blend of rage and curiosity. "How do you mean?"

"Well, it looks like he was killed in a avalanche." Only his once handsome face still showed.

Penn, seized with remorse at what he'd done, tried to close the remaining dead eye. The lid flipped back open. He tried again. The corpse continued to stare. Ram stood with his hands on his hips, as if he'd personally accomplished a great task. He looked around the peaceful, winter woods. "Hey guys, look! There's buds on them trees—in January!"

Miles away, as Danni herded the kids inside from recess, she saw a robin plucking up a worm. The January thaw had come.

ABOUT THE AUTHOR

K. Marvin Bruce has studied in western Pennsylvania, eastern Massachusetts, and southern Scotland. He has taught mythology and folklore in Wisconsin and New Jersey. He has published twenty-eight fiction stories in a variety of venues. His work has been nominated for a Pushcart Prize, the Write Well Award (Silver Pen Writers Association), and the Best of the Web Award, and has won prizes from *Calliope, Danse Macabre,* and *Typehouse Literary Magazine.*

TREATMENT

ERIC REITAN

They descend
relentless as eagles swooping
to reclaim their eggs

The premiere of his treasonous poem began as a festival. The crowd at the Great Amphitheater overflowed onto the grassy hill, humming with excitement to hear the Poet Laureate of Earth. Judas wasn't quite sure where this celebrity came from. His poems about loss were born of second-hand feelings, more pity than pathos. But somehow, amidst too much death, they'd struck a chord.

Now he struck another; or perhaps it was a hammer blow he struck. As he read the poem the festival mood begin to fade. Adoration withered on a thousand faces.

As the last couplet ceased to echo, a single voice hurled out his name like a curse.

As a child he hadn't known. On official documents it was J David Smith, just the "J" without elaboration.

"What does it mean?" he'd asked his parents once.

His mother turned away red-faced. "Ask your father."

Daddy shrugged as if it were a trifle. "The day before you were born the preacher said we all should bear the betrayer's name. In our hearts, none are better than him."

And now, with a poem, he'd restored to his name its original resonance. In the silence between that shouted "Judas!" and the arrival of the EarthForce peacekeepers, he read the crowd, looking for something else amidst the expressions of dismay and betrayal. Something he was praying for. A different kind of shattering.

\#\#\#

His interrogator's face was round, almost kindly. The brown eyes were warm. According to the placards on the wall, Dr. Claude Veritas was a graduate of the prestigious Hanfield Institute of Psychiatric Medicine and a Colonel in the EarthForce Medical Corps.

"You know," Judas said, "if you want to convey the illusion that you're a real therapist, you might consider a beard."

"I'll keep it in mind. Your parents called you David, yes?"

"That's right."

"So when did you decide to go by your first name?"

"When I started college I had my friends call me Judas."

"Why?"

Judas smiled. "Careful, Dr. Veritas. You're beginning to talk like a real therapist."

"Maybe that's what I am."

"Speaking of names, is Veritas an Orwellian joke?"

Veritas riffled through the folder in front of him. "I think you misunderstand. I'm not here to brainwash you. I'm here to explore the *possibility* that your views are...born of something other than insight."

"Like some deep, subconscious urge to live down to my name."

"So why did you decide to go by Judas?"

"Didn't anyone ever tell you what Christianity's about? It's about being straight. If you're gay you might as well have nailed Jesus to the cross yourself."

"I detect bitterness."

"I guess your years of psychological training have paid off."

"Have you had contact with your parents since you came out?"

"I received an excommunication letter from their church. Obviously my father's work."

"What did it say?"

"I think the fires of perdition were mentioned."

"I see. How did that make you feel?"

"Did you really need to ask *that*? You could've said, 'Why do you think your father wrote the letter?' Work on your creativity. You're talking to a poet here."

Veritas chuckled. "When did you get the idea that the powerglobes were eggs?"

"As a gay man I'm *obsessed* with reproduction. Can't make babies, so I can't stop thinking about them. It's only natural I'd look at the globes and see little baby aliens powering the Earth."

"Judas, let's not be disingenuous. You *can* make babies. You just choose not to."

Judas laughed.

Veritas's mouth twitched as if he were trying not to join him. But then he sighed. "Do you think EarthForce hasn't studied the globes? If there were little aliens inside, wouldn't EarthForce know?"

"Of course they know."

"Judas. The Kraals are the most dangerous enemy humanity has ever faced. If it were as simple as giving back a bunch of eggs, don't you think we'd do it?"

"The powerglobes mean limitless clean energy. We're addicted."

Veritas tapped his bottom lip. "I love Clementine oranges. I eat several a day. There's no shortage, and they're healthy. Am I an *addict*?"

"That depends."

"On what?"

"On whether the citrus farms use slave labor."

Veritas shook his head. "All you have are poetic hunches, Judas."

"The Kraals came fifty years to the day after the Explorer Five brought the powerglobes home. The Kraals are slower than us. Fifty years slower than the Explorer Five. And every attack targets the globes. They don't destroy them. They *seize* them. They're *reclaiming their young*."

"That's one *theory*, Judas. Here's another. The globes are an energy source. Nothing more. But while the Explorer Five was off saving the world, they got the attention of some nasty aliens. Maybe the Kraals *eat* the globes.

Or maybe they want to eat *us*, and the focus on the globes is tactical. Take them away and our throats are *bared*." Veritas fixed Judas with a hard stare. "Your parents rejected you, Judas. It must be *nice* to think of parents who'll travel all the way across the galaxy to save their young."

Judas shifted in his cell. A single bulb, secured behind a steel grate, blazed over his cot. It was powered by a generator outside the city, probably adjacent to one of the old coal plants that, in an earlier age, had spewed carbon dioxide into the skies. The new generator would be quiet, clean, with a single powerglobe at its heart and a ring of EarthForce troops surrounding it. They'd be armed with Kraal-killers—each weapon powered by a single globe.

Take them away and our throats are bared.

He wouldn't be surprised if, at their next interview, Veritas invoked Pascal's Wager.

It was the obvious move, and so far Veritas had been nothing but obvious. He'd seen the ploy about his parents' rejection coming before the interview even started. And yet, somehow, he couldn't stop thinking about *them*, about his childhood, about the red swing in the yard. Some of his earliest memories were of Daddy swinging him while singing silly songs. At its highest forward arc the swing carried him to the kitchen window, and on summer afternoons he'd see Mommy at the stove, her hair in a bun, her brow furrowed as she studied some recipe.

At bedtime it was Mommy who stroked his brow. "God watch over you in the night and keep you safe, little one." But on nights when he couldn't sleep, he'd call for Daddy. Daddy would sit by the bed and sing: "Jesus loves me, this I know."

You have chosen the path that leads to death. You have set your life against His will. For the good of the whole this evil must be put from our sight.

Judas remembered holding the letter, resisting the urge to crumple it as he read his father's words. He remembered Daddy's steady hands on the swing, pushing with endless patience while little David cried out, "Faster! Faster!"

Back then he was David even in his own heart.

Judas rubbed his forehead. He thought about saying nothing. With the constant glaring light in his cell, he wasn't sleeping well. He knew enough about brainwashing to know that was part of it.

But conversations went two ways. Veritas wasn't the only one here with power. "Can't you hear their screams?"

"Screams?"

"They've gotten worse since we invented the Kraal-killers."

"Those sonic booms are a *terror tactic*. They can't attack us directly anymore, so they terrorize us from the skies."

"Think, Veritas. A single globe can power a city for decades. But each Kraal-killer drains a globe in three blasts. They've stopped their attacks because they don't want their children to die."

"Another poet's theory." Veritas glanced at a paper on his desk. "I see you studied philosophy in college." Veritas looked up from the paper. "Ever read Pascal's Wager?"

Judas couldn't help himself. He started to laugh, and it became a manic thing. It wasn't funny, but his body heaved and his head throbbed, and every time he tried to stop, to say a word, the laughter came convulsively again.

And he thought about his father's anger. It had been a contained thing except that one time when his mother was in the hospital. For a week Daddy had been feeding him sandwiches, frozen pizza, precooked noodle dishes. On the seventh day, while Daddy was getting ready to ladle macaroni, David imagined vomiting all over his father's plate. Saucy noodles plopped down and David watched his father, imagining that he was eating vomit. The manic laughter started on its own.

"Stop it," Daddy hissed.

But David couldn't stop. He saw his father's growing rage but there was nothing he could do. Daddy's chair crashed backwards and David kept on laughing, the mania shaking him even as his father seized him by the shirt and dragged him from the table.

When the blow came, the pain wasn't what finally stilled the laughter. What made it stop was the look on his father's face: the horror as he backed away, staring at his hand.

It was the memory of his father's self-loathing that brought the laughter under control. Judas held the image of it behind his closed eyes, like an image a Buddhist would focus on to still the mind. He wiped away the tears. He met Veritas' kindly eyes. "I never was a fan of Pascal's Wager."

Veritas cocked his head. If Judas were to guess, he'd say the man's puzzled look was genuine. "We don't know who's right." Veritas said it carefully, as if expecting his words to set off another explosion of mania. "So we have to bet. We have to go with the *safest* bet." He leaned forward, and his voice gained momentum as if he were reassured by Judas' silence. "What if we go with your theory, bet that the powerglobes are baby Kraals, and we're wrong? It would mean *the end of the world*. If we bet the other way, we fight a war we can win. Even if we're wrong, what have we lost?"

It was as if Veritas were setting him up. Maybe he was: drawing him in with a calculated show of weakness. But Judas only had one move.

"Our souls," he said.

Veritas gazed at him steadily.

Judas pressed on. "Do we risk being compassionate fools, or moral monsters? Socrates said it thousands of years ago. 'It's better to suffer wrong than to do wrong.'"

Veritas blinked. "My God," he said. "You're still a Christian, aren't you?"

"No."

"Love your enemy, even if it means the end of the world. *You want your parents to take you back.*"

"This isn't about my parents."

"I have news for you, Judas. The only way your parents will take you back is if you start screwing girls."

He'd been lying in his cell for hours, staring at the ceiling, when he felt the rumbling. His cot rattled against the wall and the bulb winked out. He sat up, blinking into the blackness.

It was delicious. The pleasure of it—of the darkness—made him shudder. He sank back down. When sleep came it was as if he were sinking out of his own body, out the back of his head, through the cot and the floor, sinking into the rich, welcoming earth.

Then the lights blazed on again.

###

"I want to show you something."

There was a monitor perched on a rolling stand. Veritas pressed a remote and chaos filled the screen. A city on fire. Rioting. *Giant space lobsters* ripping through the streets. It's what the tabloids called them. Journalists had always been bad poets.

"Last week a dozen Kraals dove into the Atlantic. Yesterday they came up again. The ground turned molten beneath the soldiers' feet. At a dozen power plants around the world. At the same moment. The damned things bored their way up through the earth. The soldiers were roasted before there was even a target for their Kraal-killers. And then the damned monsters snatched up the powerglobes and launched themselves back into space. Except the two that decided to slag New York City on their way out."

Judas watched the images of devastation. He'd seen it all before, but not enough to make him numb.

Veritas turned off the screen and returned to his desk. "There's a damned *movement*, Judas. Three million dead in New York, and there's a movement to give the Kraals what they want. Hand over the globes and hope for the best. It'll be our death."

"Or salvation."

Veritas snorted. "Your father's religion is in your bones, Judas. Except you want to *be* Christ."

"I'm a poet. I want to speak the truth."

"The only difference between prophets and fanatics is that the fanatics are *wrong*." He paused, studying Judas' face. "People are afraid, Judas. They think EarthForce has failed, and even the wildest poet's theories are looking good. Someone's put your damned poem to *music*, for God's sake. Not very good, though. Sounds too much like *Home on the Range*."

Judas laughed. But the vision of Manhattan, a city in flames, remained. And he could see his father, hands raised over his head, brow furrowed. He could almost hear the words of the prayer, fervent and sure.

"You want something from me."

Veritas sighed. "An MP in the World Parliament has taken up the so-called *Judas' Solution* and is pushing it hard. Before yesterday people laughed at him. Today he has a following. Tomorrow..." Veritas shrugged. "EarthForce is designing a new weapon, something that should turn the tide of this war. But it's useless without the powerglobes." Veritas paused. "A disavowal from you—now, before this takes on more momentum—might be enough."

"They'll say I've been brainwashed."

"Don't tell the world you're wrong. Admit you *might* be. Ask the world how they want to *bet*."

Veritas picked up the remote and turned the monitor back on. Judas didn't want to watch, but he couldn't help it. The spokes of Liberty's crown were just cresting the thrashing waters. He pressed his fingernails into his palms to suppress a burst of manic laughter.

"You might want to know," Veritas said, "that your father was in New York City on business when it happened. He hasn't been heard from since the attack."

###

"Our God is an awesome God, son. He reigns in heaven above with wisdom, power, and love. And He hears your prayers. Do you hear me, David? He hears them, and he knows what's in your heart. These feelings have been put in you by Satan. To indulge them is..." David's father closed his eyes and shuddered. "Every time you...you do what you do, *Satan* is your lover!" When his eyes flew open again, they shone with tears. "Open your heart to Christ, David. He'll cleanse you."

"I've tried that every day since I was twelve."

"No. You haven't. God reads the deepest wishes of your heart. A part of you refuses to give it over to God."

"How can you possibly know that?"

"Because you haven't changed!"

David felt it, that moment when everything went cold inside him and he knew his world would never be the same. "Damn you to hell, Father."

###

It was his mother's voice. Judas wedged the crude flip-phone more firmly under his chin and glared at the orderly in the doorway. "Why are you calling me?"

"Your father's dead."

Judas said nothing.

"He was on the ferry. He...wanted to see the statue. He was talking to me on the phone when it started."

"And you're calling me? Father wouldn't approve."

He could hear her sob. He thought about snapping the phone shut and handing it back to the orderly.

"You're just like him," she said.

"I'm *nothing* like him." He knew it wasn't true. "I'm sorry for you."

"He was so stubborn. He'd rather cut off his own son than be wrong. But I believe—I believe it, David—I believe he would've come around."

"Guess we'll never know."

###

His Daddy died two weeks after David's sixth birthday, on the Sunday the new pastor came. David was sitting in the back pew, flanked by his parents, when the thick-set preacher told the congregation about his dream. "I saw someone with eyes half-open, a man whose heart belongs halfway to

31

Christ. I saw him poised between a lukewarm faith and true commitment. A good man, but a man afraid to give his whole heart.

"Christ appeared to me in my dream and said this man would be here today, here in *this* church. He told me to invite him forward, to invite him into the bosom of Christ." The preacher paused. His hands had been raised, his eyes closed, but now he lowered his arms and swept his gaze over the congregation. "Who is this man?"

In the silence that followed, David's Daddy rose and jostled his way to the center aisle. He walked forward, and the preacher raised his arms and called upon the name of the Lord. David watched the frenzied prayer that followed. His Daddy swooned and fell into the preacher's meaty arms.

His father said he'd been born anew, but David knew it was death. Daddy no longer sang to him. It was prayers now, prayers with one hand in the air. The compassion in his eyes had been burned away by conviction, and all that remained was Father.

Daddy was gone.

And so David decided it was time to die, too. He'd be Judas.

"You killed him."

Judas sighed and rubbed his temples. "I'd expect more subtlety from you, Veritas. Make *me* think it. What are they *teaching* you guys at EarthForce interrogation training these days?"

"Not that it matters anymore, but it's psycho-indoctrination, not interrogation."

Judas looked at Veritas. The man's face looked harrowed. "And here I thought we've been having a philosophical debate."

Veritas let out a growl. "You're not even a very good poet."

Judas raised an eyebrow. "Is this some new strategy? The *insult* technique?"

"You don't get it, do you? This isn't a game. It's the *fate of the world.*"

Judas sat up straighter. "You're a true believer, aren't you?"

Veritas didn't answer.

Judas shook his head. "Even if the World Parliament votes to hand over the powerglobes, do you really think EarthForce will *comply*?"

"Of course not."

Judas blinked. And then he saw it, the deeper thrust of Veritas's meaning. Judas had said the words himself. Not even a *common enemy*, not even the threat of *annihilation*, could unite a bickering humanity. *Too many poets causing dissension in the ranks.*

Judas imagined EarthForce turning its guns on the World Parliament. He imagined the Eastern Bloc, suspicious of EarthForce and its agendas, raising an army to oppose the coup. And the Kraals, waiting above. "Maybe I need to write another poem."

"What'll you write?"

Judas rubbed his eyes. "Something about my father."

###

It was the first thing he saw when his cell door opened. It sat on his cot, the size of a golf ball. "What's *that* doing here?"

The orderly didn't reply. When Judas didn't move, the man shoved him into the cell and slammed the door.

Judas stared at it. His tongue felt thick. In all his life he'd never before seen anything but pictures.

In truth, it looked very much like an egg.

Finally he went to it and picked it up. It was heavy for its size. A thrill went through him. The photographs had never fully captured the *color* of the egg.

It was a color he couldn't forget. He'd seen the Kraals when they'd attacked the power station outside Salt Lake City. He'd been hiking in the hills, and one of them had soared close, the sun shining off its enormous carapace. Like silvery milk.

"My God." He closed his fist around it.

Why put it here, into his hands? Proof of all his speculations. It warmed in his grip. He could almost feel the life stirring within.

He'd grown used to tuning out the screams, but he heard them now: distant roars of power and pain rumbling down from heaven.

"You're the one who named them, aren't you? Kraals."

"I'm good with names. What is it you *want,* Veritas?"

"There were twenty more attacks last night. And while EarthForce was distracted, they hit Paris. Millions dead. And the Louvre..." Veritas closed his eyes. "It's gone, Judas. The *Mona Lisa.* Caravaggio's *Death of the Virgin.*"

"Flandrin's *Nude Youth Sitting by the Sea.* I get it, Veritas." Judas' hand was in his pocket. He couldn't get himself to leave it behind. Or leave it alone. He turned it in his fingers. "What do you want me to say? If you want to save the Uffizi, *give back the globes.*"

Veritas sighed. "There are four stages to psycho-indoctrination. With a receptive patient, you can get past the first stage in a matter of days."

"What's your point?"

"There isn't *time.* If you're going to recant, you've got to do it *now.*"

Judas stared. He saw the twitch of Veritas' left eye. "You know that's not going to happen. Not after I've seen the globe."

Veritas fixed Judas with a sharp gaze. "The vote is tomorrow. Mandate 2136.87B. *Judas' Solution.* How does that make you feel?"

"If it happens," Judas said, "if they really give them up, it will be...a vindication."

"Mass delusion isn't going to *vindicate* you. It'll just prove that desperation can drive an entire civilization insane."

Maybe that's what happened to the Kraals. "I wasn't talking about vindicating myself," he said. "I was talking about humanity."

"Your father's *dead,* Judas. You've got nothing left to prove to him."

"This isn't about my father."

Veritas snorted. "The World Parliament has requested a written statement. Your words. *Whatever you want to say.* It'll be read on the parliament floor before the vote."

Judas blinked. "Someone's…what? Protecting me?"

Veritas snorted again. "Of course. Had my hands not been tied—believe me, Judas, you're not nearly as clever as you think. You'd be standing on the parliament floor tomorrow, reciting a poem to stir the soul. A poem about unity, about standing together to *fight* when real evil descends from the skies. And you'd believe *every word.*"

Judas was trembling when the monitor was brought into his cell. He'd spent most of the night writing what he needed to say. Not a poem. Just words.

Judas cupped the globe in his hands as he watched the screen. "Any minute now," he said to it. In his cell it had been easy to start talking to it, imagining the life within.

A woman with silver hair approached the central podium. The parliament seats were ranged about like pews. The woman's face was gaunt, parchment stretched over a skull. He didn't recognize her. "The words of Judas Smith," she said.

I've held a globe. They are the stuff of the Kraals, the same milky stuff of power. We love our children with a ferocity that leaves no room for compromise. When we look at ourselves we see frail human flesh and the reality of sin. But when we look at our children we see the breath of God, and we are astonished. And we want them, always, to be that thing we see in them, the thing that gives us hope. In our children we see the promise of our own redemption. This is why, so often, fathers grow to hate their sons, and mothers weep at their daughters' failures. And it is why we protect them so fiercely. It is why the loss of our children is an affliction almost beyond imagining. As it is with us, so it is with the Kraals.

The woman stepped down from the podium, and the voting began.

Judas held the globe almost tenderly when the results were announced. He found himself rocking where he sat. And then, for the first time, he was crying for the Daddy he'd lost too many times.

Judas was led into the bright sun of a crisp fall day. An EarthForce jeep waited at the door, blocking his view of the tarmac. Soldiers shoved him into the back of it. Veritas sat on a bench inside, his face expressionless. Judas sat down opposite him, flanked by two soldiers.

"Where are we going?"

"To witness the fruits of your labors." Veritas smiled, a tight smile that concealed something. Anger? No. Nothing so simple.

The jeep rumbled into motion. The back window was open, admitting brisk dusty air. Judas sat in silence. *The fruits of my labors.* The monitor had remained in his cell, and he'd been allowed to watch the reports as the globes were gathered up, as cities went dark. Old nuclear facilities were firing up, and the World Parliament claimed to have a plan for renovating the abandoned coal generators. Scientists assured the public that studies of the globes had yielded extraordinary insights, that viable alternatives were only a few years away.

It was all announced with cheerful enthusiasm. But the audience grew smaller as the world was descending into darkness, and even the news anchors' smiles couldn't hide the birth pangs of chaos.

But the Kraal attacks had stopped. So had the screaming from the skies. Somehow the Kraals understood. He imagined them waiting, enormous and impenetrable, for their children to be gathered up.

"We're going there," Judas said. "Aren't we? To the place where they're being collected."

Veritas offered a curt nod.

No one had come for his globe. It rested still in his pocket, and it would travel with him now to the gathering place in the Mojave Desert, to be added to the vast and precious offering.

Judas looked at Veritas. "Why didn't they fight it?"

"What?"

"Where's the coup? The civil war?" In fact, the gathering of the globes had all the efficiency of a military operation.

Veritas smiled thinly. "Maybe you convinced them."

Judas fingered his own globe. That's how he thought of it: *his own*. It felt warmer than it had before.

He wasn't fool enough to think a poet's words had moved EarthForce high command. "The Eastern Bloc," he said. "They did something."

Veritas shrugged. "Something like that."

Judas sat in silence. And then he remembered sitting in Veritas's office, and Veritas speaking with fierceness in his eyes: *EarthForce is designing a new weapon, something that should turn the tide of this war.* Judas felt a sudden chill. *My God.* He looked up and met Veritas' gaze.

Veritas' eyes widened a fraction. "Crap. Take his globe." The soldiers next to Judas looked up. "Take it NOW!"

Judas was seized from both sides. He tried to fight, but these were trained soldiers. Their arms were steel. They yanked away the globe, even as he cried out.

"Out the window! Now!"

The globe flew out the back of the jeep. Judas staggered after. He clutched the rear window's low sill, looked back into the dust cloud, trying to see its silvery gleam. He felt as if his heart had been torn out.

"It's how they know." Veritas' voice was calm again. "They need direct contact. Skin to skin. They read our thoughts."

"I..." Judas stared out the back of the jeep. He was about to say he didn't understand. But he did. "The new weapon," he whispered. "All the globes...all of them in one place...are they *bait*? Or the power source." He was still staring out the back of the jeep, fruitlessly searching for the globe.

"Both." A small laugh. "I doubt we could've done it without you, Judas. You may have saved the world after all."

Judas thought he saw a glimmer through the dust. His heart skipped. He rubbed his eyes. An illusion born of hope? But no. There it was again. Growing larger, and not just because it was drawing near.

It was *unfolding*. Petals of milky silver blossomed outward, growing more beautiful as he watched. Manic laughter threatened to bubble up, but he swallowed it down. "Too late, I think." He turned to Veritas.

Veritas looked at him. "What?"

Judas smiled. "They're hatching."

Dr. Eric Reitan is a philosophy professor at Oklahoma State University, where he specializes in ethics and the philosophy of religion. His short fiction has appeared in numerous venues including *The Magazine of Fantasy and Science Fiction, Gamut, Deciduous Tales,* and the *Alien Invasion* anthology from Flame Tree Press. He is the recipient of the Oklahoma Writers Federation's Crème-de-la-Crème award, the Rose State Outstanding Writer award, and fourth place in the 2019 Writers' Digest Short Story Competition. His academic books include *Is God a Delusion?* (Wiley-Blackwell, 2009), which was named a Choice Outstanding Academic Title. *The Triumph of Love: Same-Sex Marriage and the Christian Love Ethic* (Cascade, 2017) is his most recent book.

FORESEEABLE

PAUL LEVINSON

They sometimes call bathrooms washrooms, right? Anyway, I went into the bathroom – the men's room – in Saggio's just to wash my hands and face. It was a hot July day in the city, I'd walked from the train at 181st Street, and I wanted to be as fresh as possible for Jenny. We'd known each other for a while, ever since the Psych Class we'd taken at NYU almost a year ago, but this was just our second date, and I very much wanted everything to go right.

I got back to our table. I'd arrived at the restaurant about ten minutes early – unusual for me – and kept my eye on the door for Jenny. I realized I couldn't see that clearly--Of course not, stupid me, I'd left my glasses in the washroom. I got up and rushed back in.

Ah, there they were! Right on the nice marbled sink, where I'd left them. I had a pair of black horn-rimmed glasses – what can I tell you – and they were right there. I picked them up and knew that they weren't mine a split second later. A little heavier, the black was a subtler shade, I don't know. But they weren't mine.

I dashed out of the washroom and looked around the restaurant. It wasn't that big. Most of the tables were filled. A few guys had on glasses, but none were even remotely like mine. Several were wire rimmed. One was like Buddy Holly's, black, but otherwise not like mine. What was going on?

I sat down at my table, and I know this was another dumb thing to do, but I put on the pair of glasses I'd found in the men's room. And they worked for me, perfectly! Of course they did – the guy who had mistakenly taken mine must have thought they were his, because our prescriptions were the same. My vision's not that bad – I'm just a little near-sighted – and there must be a huge number of glasses with my prescription out there.

I looked at the door. Everything was crystal clear. Including Jenny, who walked in, looking great in a soft blue tank top and washed-out jeans. I stood, smiling, and waved her over to my table.

"You've got new glasses," she said, and gave me a big smile back.

"Yeah," I said. I thought at lightning speed. No, I wasn't going to tell how I had gotten these glasses, at least, not now. Maybe after we'd gotten to know each other better.

The waiter came over with menus. I took my glasses off and put them in my shirt pocket. They got in the way of my reading, and I didn't like wearing them when I was eating, either.

Dinner was delicious. So was the conversation. Jenny excused herself to go to the lady's room, and I signaled the waiter for the check. I got it quickly and paid with my phone. I had just put my glasses back on when Jenny returned.

"You ok?" she asked. "You look like you've just seen a ghost." She laughed, a little.

"Fine," I assured her and stood. "I was just ... thinking about something."

"Ok," she said. "You can tell me about it on the way home. Should we take the train?" She had a nice little apartment in the village – her parents paid for it, their way of keeping her in New York – and her saying I should accompany her on the trip back home probably meant I had a pretty good chance of being invited up there.

"Sure," I said. "But why don't we walk a little first. You in the mood for that?"

She nodded. "It's cooled off a little. What could be better than a walk near the Hudson River in the summer?"

***

We walked along the bike path, and it was indeed beautiful. But now I'd lied to Jenny about two things. One, a lie of omission about how I'd obtained these new glasses. Two, that I was thinking about something when she came back from the lady's room.

The truth was, I hadn't been thinking about something. I'd been *seeing* something. The southbound A train stalled just out of the station, the one near our restaurant. I hadn't imagined that or envisioned it or anything like that. It wasn't a day dream. I had actually seen it – and Jenny and me stuck, irritated, frustrated on that stalled train.

I went in to speak to Jim the next day. He was a PhD student in psychology – a grad assistant in our program – and seemed the best person I knew to talk about hallucinations, even though I was still sure I had not been hallucinating.

I told him about what had happened to me the night before. I told him everything, including about my new glasses – who knows, maybe they were putting some strain on my brain. I also told him that I'd checked online and there had indeed been some huge delay in the subway near Washington Heights, which is just where Jenny and I had been the night before. Ok, I didn't tell him one thing, that I'd spent the night at Jenny's and it had been great, after we'd walked about twenty blocks and caught an IRT train which was running fine and stopped right across the street from her apartment. But that had happened after my vision of the stalled train and was none of his business besides.

"So your vision about the train proved to be true," Jim said. "That's why you're so concerned about this."

"Exactly."

"Well, there is such a thing as coincidence, but I agree that what you saw was very specific," he said.

"Right."

"What were you doing right before you saw this?"

"I was waiting for Jenny to come back from the lady's room and was idly looking at the front of the restaurant," I replied.

"And you put back on your newly acquired glasses?"

"Yes," I said.

"And the first time you ever had an experience like this was last night, after you got the glasses? Seeing something slightly in the future."

"Yes," I said. "I'm certain I never had an experience like that before."

"Well, then, the glasses are definitely the significant variable – the factor that either made you lose your mind, but with pinpoint accuracy, or gave you a glimpse of your future," Jim said.

"That's what I was thinking," I said. "But which one? Crazy or seeing the future?"

"That's the question," Jim said. "And it may not matter, since, crazy or not, you apparently actually did see the future. Which would be a huge coincidence if you also were crazy." Jim stroked his beard. "Do you have the new glasses with you?"

I reached into my shirt pocket and pulled out the glasses. "I do."

"Mind if I see them?" Jim asked.

I thought for a hard second. "Sure." I handed Jim the glasses. I'd nearly said, "be careful with them," but figured that might be insulting.

Jim did handle the glasses very carefully. He held them up to the light that was coming through the window, slowly opened and closed the arms, set the glasses on the table with the arms folded and scrutinized them. "Is it ok with you if I try them on?"

"I ... sure, I guess so," I replied. "You want to see if they have that same effect on you? I've had them on several times this morning, and saw nothing strange."

Jim nodded and carefully donned the glasses. "I have close to perfect vision," he said. He took the glasses off and shook his head. "All I saw was a blur." He gave the glasses back to me.

"So what's our next step?" I asked.

He laughed. "Well, you do have me intrigued. The next step would be to take account of all the variables that could have been at play at the time of your vision."

"We go back to Saggio's?" I asked.

"Yep, and the same time of day would be good. And with your girlfriend there, too."

"How do we account for the same patrons who were there last night?" I asked.

Jim shook his head. "We can't account for everything."

***

I realized I had to be honest with Jenny, and own up completely to the lies I had told her the night before. She had asked something about the glasses again, after we'd made love last night, and I'd given her some kind of vague answer that I couldn't quite remember. We were both pretty hammered and more than half asleep by then. But, yeah, one-hundred percent disclosure was called for now. There was no other way I could reasonably ask her to come back to the very same restaurant we had dined in last night, and have Jim join us no less, without telling her exactly how I'd really gotten hold of these glasses, and, even more importantly, what I had seen through them.

I sat down on a bench in Washington Square Park to think things out. But I didn't get much thinking done. There was a band on the far side of the park doing acoustic covers of some of my favorite Beatles songs with spot-on, perfect harmonies. There was always a comfort in hearing Beatles harmony, and I sure needed some of that now. I sang along, under my breath, and put on my glasses so I could get a better look at the group.

That was my mistake. Within seconds after I had put on my glasses, I saw not the group, but Jenny and me, in her apartment. Neither of us was happy. She was telling me that trust was the most important thing to her, and how could she trust me, seeing as how I had lied to her so blatantly last night. "Why didn't you tell me the truth?"

"I thought you'd think I was a weirdo," I said.

She frowned. "How do I know you're telling me the truth right now?"

I took my glasses off and slowly exhaled. So now these glasses had gotten me into an even worse bind. They had shown me that maybe it wasn't a good idea to confide in Jenny, even though I just had decided that it was. Telling her what was going on still seemed the best way of getting her to come back with me to the restaurant. But the glasses had shown me that this was a path that led to further aggravation, before we ever got back to the restaurant.

Well, maybe I'd a least learned one welcome thing from this second vision. This made two out of two visions in which Jenny and I were the subjects. Was she somehow connected to my seeing slightly into the future?

I messaged Jim and told him what had happened. He told me he could meet me on the park bench in 45 minutes. I waked slowly to Sixth Avenue and got a latte.

***

Jim was on the bench when I returned, with someone else who looked a little older than he was, a redhead. She stood along with Jim and gave me a bright smile. "This is Peg," Jim introduced her. "A friend of mine from Columbia. She has a dual appointment in Physics and Philosophy. Is it ok if she joins us?"

"Yes," I said, and shook her extended hand. "I appreciate the additional help."

"I've been working like a demon on a biography of Morgenbesser," Peg said. "I appreciate the break."

"I don't think I know his work," I said.

"He was a philosopher at Columbia," Jim said, "from, what, the 1960s through the 90s?"

"Close enough," Peg replied.

"Sorry I didn't ask if you wanted any coffee or tea," I said. I was just about finished with mine.

"We're fine," Jim said, and gestured me to sit. "So, to the matter at hand ..."

I sat and nodded.

"We were thinking it would be very helpful if you could see if your second vision is true," Jim said, "like you did with the first one."

"But, unfortunately, there's no independent source of action, like the trains in your first vision," Peg said. "If you go to see your friend, now—"

"Jenny," I supplied.

"Right, Jenny, thanks," Peg said. "But if you go see Jenny now, and tell her about how you got your glasses, and your two future visions, one of them, the first one, with the two of you essentially bystanders, the second, with the two of you as the only players having a tense moment, well—"

"There'd be no way of knowing if the tense moment was somehow brought on by what you saw in your vision, and you therefore were more anxious to begin with, because of that," Jim said. "Circular, impossible to separate cause and effect. That kind of anxiety can be contagious, self-escalating."

"And if it went the other way, that you were more careful with how you broke this news to her," Peg continued, "and as a result the two of had no discord, just a good talk, then that wouldn't prove anything, either. Maybe your knowledge from your vision diffused the situation, and that's why the talk went well, or maybe your vision was not a true vision of the future after all."

I sighed. "So, either way, we would have no way of knowing if my vision through the glasses of Jenny and me in the slight future was accurate," I said. "I get it. So, what do we do?"

"I think we've eliminated Saggio's as a significant variable," Jim said. "Your second vision didn't take place in that restaurant."

"That's true if the second vision was true," I said. "You two just convinced me that there's no way we can know that."

Peg smiled. "You're right, he's sharp," she said to Jim about me. To me she said: "And you're right, too. We can't know with any certainty if your second vision was an accurate glimpse of the future, but I'm willing to assume it's true, for now, and see where that takes us."

"Ok," I said. "So again, what's our next move?"

"Might I see the glasses?" Peg asked.

***

She examined them much the way that Jim had done, but didn't ask to put them on, and she handed them back to me. "Light goes through glass, obviously," she said, "and now I'm putting on my physicist hat."

"Ok," I said and put the glasses back in my shirt pocket.

"It can bend light – refract light is the technical term – it can refract light, it can also reflect light, it can do all sorts of things with light," Peg said.

"The question is whether it can show someone light, or something light is shining on, from the future," Jim said.

"I believe it can," I said. "But why only me? It did nothing for Jim when he tried them on at our earlier meeting in his office."

"Light is very much a part of quantum mechanics," Peg said, "and quantum mechanics is about the power of individual minds to influence physical states."

"So you're saying that my visions of the future through these glasses might be a combination of some kind of light-bending that these glasses do, when *my* eyes are looking through them, because my eyes are connected to my brain which is in some kind of synch with this light-bending on a quantum level? Wow!"

"Wow indeed," Peg said.

"How could we test that hypothesis?" I asked.

"Well, neither Peg nor I spotted anything unusual in the glass when we eyeballed it," Jim said, "but it could be examined with all kinds of higher power electron transition microscopes that should tell us more."

"I'd have to give over these glasses to a laboratory?" I asked, though the answer was obvious.

Jim and Peg both nodded.

"I'm not sure I'd want to do that," I said,

"We thought you'd feel that way," Jim said.

"At least not until I learn more about this, and what role Jenny is playing, likely unaware that she's playing it," I said. Then added, "although for all I know she is aware."

"Agreed," Peg said. "So let's get back to what we can do so you can learn more about the glasses and Jenny's role in what you've been seeing."

"Ok," I said. "You know that there's another possibility that we didn't mention. Let's say I just don't go over to see Jenny at all today? That would be one way of eliminating the dispute I saw."

"We've already established that if you see something in the near future, and change your current behavior based on that vision, what you saw won't happen," Peg replied. "That what's happened with the vision of Jenny and you stuck on the train last night. Because of that vision, you got Jenny to walk twenty blocks with you and avoided that train. That would be the same effect if, as a result of your vision of you and Jenny today, you didn't go over to see her."

"I see what you're saying," I said.

"And I have yet another idea, another permutation on this visit today," Jim said. "How about all three of us pay Jenny a visit? That would enable you to tell her about your lies of omission and commission last night, and Peg and I could observe the reaction and how it played out."

"Always good to have extra observers in a strange situation like this,"
Peg said.

"So now Jenny's a guinea pig?"

"You had to know that could happen when you came to talk to me about
this in the first place," Jim said.

***

The three of us walked over to Jenny's apartment. It was maybe a 10-
minute walk from where we were, on the other side of Sixth Avenue.   I'd
called her on the phone, told her I had a psychologist and a philosopher-
physicist friend I wanted her to meet, and she said sure, anything beat this
paper she was trying to write. Once again, I told her nothing about the glasses.
I guess this made the third lie I'd foisted on her about the glasses, another lie
of omission. I was getting tired of counting.

The bigger regret, though, I had about going to see Jenny this way was I
knew that, if she thought it was just me coming to visit, just me and not three's
a crowd, who knows what she might be wearing, maybe next to nothing, which
is what she'd had on when I'd kissed her goodbye this morning. But I guess
these light-bending glasses took precedence over the normal pleasures of life.

We reached the corner across the street from Jenny's apartment
building.

"Why don't you put on the glasses and see if you see anything," Peg said.
"But don't tell us what, if you do."

"Good idea, another kind of check on what's going on," Jim said. "We'll
find out what happens if you get a glimpse of the future, but don't tell us."

"I did that with Jenny last night," I said.

"Right, but we're not Jenny," Jim said.

"Ok." The light turned to green, I put on the glasses, and started
walking across the street.

"Whoa," Jim said, and put a retraining arm on me. "Better wait with
the glasses until we're on the other side, not in the middle of an intersection."

I pulled off the glasses.

48

We crossed the street and stopped near a Japanese restaurant. "You can put them on now," Peg said.

I did as requested – and flinched. I removed the glasses.

"Don't tell us," Peg said. I could tell she and Jim had been watching me closely.

"Can we go see Jenny now?" I asked.

Peg and Jim nodded.

***

Jenny was wearing more than when I'd seen her this morning but she still looked great. She greeted with me a hug at the open door. I introduced Jim and Peg.

"Come in," Jenny said. We did. "This is my friend, Krystal." A woman, Jenny's age or maybe a little older, I guess, was sitting on the sofa. She rose and walked over to meet us. She had black curly hair and wore glasses with blue frames.

"I hope it's ok that I asked her to join us," Jenny said.

"Of course," Peg and Jim said.

"I work in the boutique on Sullivan Street," Krystal said. "We sell designer glasses."

"Aha! Could be useful," Peg said. She turned to me. "But I thought you said you hadn't told—"

"I'm confused," I said.

Jim touched his beard in thought. "So everyone here knows about Sven's strange glasses – how he found them, what happens sometimes when he puts them on."

"I'm not sure how—" I began.

"You told me last night," Jenny said to me, with just a touch of a mischievous smile. "Just before we fell asleep. I mean, we did have a lot to drink. Don't tell me you don't remember any of that?"

"I remember some of that," I said, embarrassed, not because of what I remembered but because of what I didn't.

"Please, sit down," Jenny said to all of us, and gestured to the sofa and some plush chairs in front of it.

We complied.

"May I ask what it is that Sven told you last night?" Peg asked Jenny. "If it's not too personal?"

"That he left his glasses in the men's room, in Saggio's, and when he realized that, and went back to the men's room, he found the new ones," Jenny replied.

"Ok, anything else?" Peg asked.

"And then later, when I went to the lady's room, he put the glasses on, and saw that the train we were going to take was stalled," Jenny said.

"You didn't find any of that creepy or crazy?" Jim asked.

"Maybe, a little," Jenny said. "I mean, it's a little icky picking up and putting on and then keeping someone else's glasses, a complete stranger's." Jenny laughed, nervously. "But, I don't know, when Sven told me, I thought maybe he was joking." She looked at me, reassuringly. "He has a good sense of humor."

I smiled at her.

"Could I see the glasses," Krystal asked.

"Sure," I said and gave her the glasses.

Krystal carefully examined them, but didn't put them on. "I don't see anything unusual about them," she said.

"That's what everyone says, other than Sven," Jim said.

"Uhm, there is one other thing," Jenny spoke up.

"Yes?" Peg said.

Krystal gave the glasses back to me and I put them in my pocket.

"I, uhm, put the glasses on this morning, when you were sleeping," she said to everyone and to me. "I would've asked you if that was ok, but you were sleeping like a baby, and I didn't want to wake you."

"That's ok," I reached over and squeezed her hand.

"And, you saw something?" Jim asked, gently, correctly guessing where Jenny was going.

"Yeah."

Everyone looked at Jenny. Her jaw was working but she didn't speak.

"That's major news," Jim finally said. "It proves what Sven's been reporting hasn't all been in his head."

Jenny nodded. "I know."

"What'd' you see?" Peg asked, not as gently as Jim.

"I saw this," Jenny replied.

"Could you be more specific?" Jim asked.

"All of us, in this room, having this exact same conversation," Jenny said. "I invited you," she said to Krystal, "because I saw you here, sitting in that exact same place, wearing what you're wearing."

"Did you catch the words in the conversation?" Peg asked.

"Yes."

"What were they?" Peg asked.

"Just what you're now saying," Jenny said. "Just what I'm saying right now – I'm losing my mind!"

I took her hand again.

Krystal stood. "I'm out of here," she said and walked to the door. "This is way above my pay grade and I have to get back to work, anyway."

No one tried to stop her as she left.

I looked at Jim and Peg. "Is that ok? That she heard all of this?"

"No one would believe her if she told them – too preposterous," Peg said.

"I barely believe it myself," Jim said.

"Has the conversation you saw ended?" Peg asked Jenny, "or did you see us still talking?"

"It ended when Krystal left," Jenny replied, slightly relieved.

"Why didn't you tell me about this, when I woke up, this morning?" I asked her.

"Because you clearly didn't know about this conversation in my vision," Jenny said. "Just like you didn't know about it a minute ago."

Peg and Jim looked like they were struggling to make sense of this. I was someplace between struggling and numb.

"Ok," Peg finally said. "So what we have here with Jenny's experience is someone *not* using the vision of the future to avoid that future – like Sven did with the train – but doing what she could to make sure her vision of the future actually came to be."

"Yeah," I said, and realized Jenny was shaking. I got next to her and put my arms around her. She started crying. "It's just too much ..." she managed to say.

I saw that Peg and Jim were both standing. "Listen, I think we've had enough for today," Jim said, looking at both of us in an older brotherly way. "I spotted a vest-pocket park about a half a block further down this street. Why don't Peg and I grab a coffee, and you can meet us there whenever you're ready."

I wasn't sure if the 'you' meant Jenny and me or just me, but I nodded, gratefully.

"Alright, good," Jim said. "We've made a lot of progress." He and Peg left.

***

Jenny's quivering had stopped and she had mostly finished crying. "I'm sorry," she said, and pulled a little away.

"It's my fault, I got you into this insanity," I said.

"Trust is the most important thing to me in a relationship," she said in a mostly clear voice. "And I lied to you. I should've told you first thing in the morning that I put on your glasses, and what I saw. And I had a chance to tell you when you called, and I didn't tell you then, either. And you lied to me, too, when it all started with that stupid train last night. Why didn't you tell me the truth?"

"I thought you'd think I was a weirdo," I said, just a split second before I realized this was the conversation I had seen when I'd put on the glasses in Washington Square Park just an hour ago. It seemed like a lifetime.

She frowned. "How do I know you're telling me the truth right now?" she asked, hoarsely.

I didn't have the power to reply.

She caught the expression on my face. "Oh my God. Don't tell me you saw this very conversation we're now having, through the glasses, earlier? You should throw those damned glasses away!"

"Peg and Jim wouldn't like that."

Jenny shook her head slowly.

"I think I have just three basic options here," I said, "give them the glasses, throw them away, or keep them."

"I'd get rid of them," Jenny said.

"I don't know," I said. "Maybe I should put them on one more time, and see if what I see can give me any guidance."

Jenny leaned over, kissed me on the lips, and put her arms around me. "Let's see if this gives you any guidance," she said and unbuttoned my shirt.

***

I wasn't really surprised to find Jim and Peg on that little park bench, right where they'd said they'd be, over an hour later. Both were sipping coffees.

"We would've gotten one for you, but it would've gotten cold already," Peg said.

"And I never asked what you were drinking in that venti," Jim added.

"It's ok, I'm fine," I said. I was the most relaxed I'd been all day.

"But it is getting late," Peg said, "and I have an appointment up at Columbia."

"We can get together again tomorrow, or later in the week, no problem," I said.

"Look, I know we asked you before if we could borrow your glasses for hi-tech examination, and you were reluctant," Peg said.

"We could get them back to you in a week, for sure," Jim said and looked at Peg.

She nodded.

"They've caused you and Jenny enough grief," Jim said. "Though it looks like you worked things out." He smiled.

"I'm going to keep them," I said, plainly.

They both almost jumped off the bench at that.

"There's a universe of scientific tests that have to be done on that glass – there's no other way to understand exactly how it bends light, so you can see what's around the bend in time," Peg said.

"You can't guarantee that such high-tech examination won't destroy the glass, and make whatever it is that bends the light inoperable, can you, though?" I asked.

"No, of course not," Peg said. "But the work will be done with the utmost of care, I can promise you."

"I'll think about it," I said. "But I want to test-drive these a little longer on my own."

They each took a step closer. Some might have called that step menacing.

But I wasn't too worried. I'd seen just a few minutes ago how this ended when I put on the glasses before I left Jenny's apartment. Just as I had seen what had made me flinch when we were on our way to Jenny.

And I now had some confidence in what I was seeing. And how I could get on top of it, and use it for my benefit and maybe even the world's benefit.

"We'll be in touch," I said and started to walk away. "I know you can't be sure of that. But I think I can."

ABOUT THE AUTHOR

Paul Levinson, PhD, is Professor of Communication & Media Studies at Fordham University in NYC. His science fiction novels include *The Silk Code* (winner of the Locus Award for Best First Science Fiction Novel of 1999), *The Consciousness Plague, The Pixel Eye, Borrowed Tides, The Plot to Save Socrates, Unburning Alexandria,* and *Chronica.* His award-nominated novelette, "The Chronology Protection Case," was made into a short film and is on Amazon Prime Video. His nonfiction books, including *The Soft Edge, Digital McLuhan, Realspace, Cellphone, McLuhan in an Age of Social Media,* and *Fake News in Real Context* have been translated into 15 languages. He appears on CBS News, CNN, MSNBC, Fox News, the Discovery Channel, National Geographic, the History Channel, and NPR. His 1972 album, *Twice Upon A Rhyme,* was re-issued in Japan and Korea in 2008, and in the U. K. in 2010. His first new album since 1972, *Welcome Up: Songs of Space and Time,* was released on Old Bear Records and Light in the Attic Records in 2020.

COMPANY

LESLIE MAXWELL KAIURA

Jason watched as Donna worked her way down the bar, wiping the polished wood in quick circles with a towel. Her curly blond ponytail bounced with the motion, and the tank top she wore under her bar apron exposed a tattoo of a red rose on her upper arm. When she reached the far end, where he had been sitting and nursing a beer for over an hour, she picked up his empty bottle and tossed it with a practiced flick of the wrist into a trash can that stood several feet away. "Can I get you another?"

"Nah, I'm good. Gotta drive home." He pulled out his wallet and put a five-dollar bill in the tip jar.

"That's twice what the beer cost. You gotta let me work for my money, hun." She gave him an inviting smile, but he wasn't quite sure what the invitation was. Southern charm? Salesmanship? Something else?

"I've been here taking up space for a while."

She laughed and looked around. It was Wednesday night, and at 9 p.m., the place was dead. "Well I don't see anybody waitin' to sit on that stool and run up a big tab. Sure you don't want one more?"

"Yeah, I'm sure. Why don't you let me buy you one instead?"

"You'd have to wait a couple of hours 'til I get off. No drinking on the job."

Jason shrugged. "Another time maybe."

"Friday I get off at nine. Julie's got the late shift."

"I guess I'll be here—maybe we can have one together after you get off."

She cocked her head to one side and rolled her eyes in a way that indicated the length the empty bar. "I'd rather get out of this place, you know."

"You do seem to spend a lot of time here."

"So do you, lately."

"It's boring at home. Too quiet."

"And this place is better?"

"At least there's company, on the nights you work, anyway."

"That's pretty sad."

"Tell me about it." She was the closest thing he had to a friend around here, and they had barely exchanged more than a little friendly bartender small talk. Yes, he was new in town. No, he didn't follow any of the teams playing basketball on the screens above the bar. She had assumed he wasn't a talker and had mostly let him be until a week or so ago, when he had left not long after her shift ended and found her in the parking lot, anxious and annoyed, trying to start a little Nissan with a dead battery. That was a problem he could fix, at least, and he had.

Donna leaned forward, and it was hard to ignore the effect created by her crossed arms and the deep neckline of her shirt. It made him a little uncomfortable. What was he doing here anyway?

"So maybe I should come over for a visit?"

"There's not much to my place, but you can come if you want."

She leaned back from the bar and laughed. "Well that's a warm invitation if I ever heard one."

"Sorry . . . I haven't had anyone over since I moved here. I haven't been in much of a social mood."

"No shit. If coming in this place to sit by yourself and have a beer or two is your idea of a social life, you need some help."

"Yeah, I guess I do." He got on okay with his boss, but he hadn't bothered to make friends since he had landed in this town on his way to nowhere. A cheap motel off the interstate, a job ad in a local paper someone had left in a booth at Aunt Edith's "Best Breakfast in Town" Diner, and here he was.

"Friday night, then?"

"I'll be here. Thanks, Donna."

"For nothing," she replied, fishing his five-dollar bill and a few singles out of the tip jar as he slid off the stool and nodded a goodbye.

The week ground on like they all had since he had answered the ad from the horse farm. The pay was low, but it came with a place to live—a little cabin where the back edge of the big property ran along the county road for a ways—and with enough hard, dirty work to wear him out. It was alright, but Friday was the fifth in a string of long days and by quitting time, it had gotten to him. The early spring weather had been chilly, but he had worked hard enough to break a sweat under his flannel shirt, and he felt disgusting. He got home, took a shower, put on a clean pair of jeans and an undershirt, and collapsed on the couch in front of the TV. He dozed off and woke up hungry, then made himself a bologna sandwich and took it and a beer back to the couch.

He had just put the empty paper plate on the floor by his feet when someone knocked on the door. A glance at his watch showed it was already twenty after nine. Dammit, he had planned to be at the bar before Donna's shift ended. He turned off the TV and got up to answer the door.

She was standing on the porch still in her work clothes—snug black jeans and a white tank top that said "Sam's Bar & Grill" across the front, the print stretched across her generous bust. The logo was only partly visible because she was hugging herself against the cold night air. For a moment he stared at her—she was almost as tall as he was, which wasn't saying much, and he couldn't avoid her eyes. She looked at him pointedly and arched an eyebrow.

"Hey, sorry." He stepped hastily to the side so that she could come in. "Really, I'm sorry. I kinda forgot we had plans."

"Well, I drive by here every day to and from work and see your old Bronco out there. It's hard to miss." She looked around the room and back at him. "Yeah, you need help."

He glanced around. It was rather pathetic. On one side of the room, there was a worn-out couch in front of a small TV on a folding tray table, and on the other side, where a dining table should have been, was his drum set. Besides those few furnishings, the work boots that he had kicked off inside the door, and the paper plate and beer bottle by the couch, the room was bare, leaving the scuffed floor and dingy walls to shine in all their run-down glory.

"I haven't settled in 'cause I wasn't sure how long I'd be here," he offered by way of explanation. "I said it wasn't much."

"I guess there's more beer in the fridge, at least?"

"Sure thing. Hold on a sec." He disappeared into the kitchen and returned with a bottle. He handed it to her and said, "I hope that's okay. If you want a glass, you'll have to settle for a Dixie cup."

"Nah, this is fine." She took a long drink before walking over and sitting down in the middle of the couch. "Good lord, it's nice to take a load off. I've been waiting tables or standing behind the bar since two this afternoon. Come sit."

Jason sat down beside her and she turned toward him, folding one foot under her other knee. She looked at him intently, resting her head against the back of the couch. He wondered how much older than him she might be. She was pretty but seemed worn around the edges.

He found that he had no idea what to say to her now that she was here. He hadn't expected her to come. Or maybe he hadn't wanted her to.

She spoke first. "So what brings you here from Georgia?"

"Georgia?"

"You still have Georgia tags on the Bronco. Saw them when I pulled up."

"Oh yeah. I just, um, needed a change."

"From what?"

"That's a long story that you probably don't wanna hear."

"Sorry, I didn't mean to pry. Just trying to make conversation."

"It's okay." He stared at the half-empty beer bottle in his hands.

Donna took the bottle from him and put it on the floor next to hers, and before it had occurred to him why she had done this, she had turned his face toward her own, leaned into him, and kissed him. She shifted closer and drew his arm around her, and for a few seconds he couldn't resist enjoying the warmth and closeness of her. But he also couldn't help thinking of Nedra, and as Donna's hand slipped through his hair to find the back of his neck, he found himself closing his eyes and wishing . . . Shit. It wasn't right. Letting her kiss him while he was thinking of someone else made him feel like even more of an asshole than usual. He broke away from her.

"I don't know what the hell I'm doing here," he said as he ran his fingers through his hair and tucked it behind his ears. He glanced over at Donna and saw that she looked confused, maybe even a little hurt. "I'm sorry. I shouldn't have . . ."

He trailed off, unsure of what to apologize for.

"No, you didn't do anything. I guess I should've known . . ."

"Known what?"

"That you weren't interested in me. You're different than most of the guys I meet at the bar. All the assholes who stare at my boobs, you know."

"Nah, I'm an asshole too," he replied, but he had to smile at her bluntness. "But I try not to stare . . . much . . . You're a sweetheart, Donna, but I'm . . ."

"Hung up on some girl back in Georgia?"

He grunted and leaned forward, elbows on knees, looking at her sidelong. "Hung up, yeah," he agreed. The words were inadequate but would do. There was a girl, and there was other shit too. Better to let her think he got dumped, but he hadn't. He had left. Hung up . . . he ought to be strung up.

"It figures . . . I meet someone who actually seems like a nice guy, and. . ."

He interrupted her. "If I was that nice, I wouldn't be here by myself with a job shoveling shit and furniture from Goodwill."

"Well, you don't have to tell me what got you here, and I'll spare you my sob story too. Sound like a deal?"

"Yeah, that sounds good."

"You mind if I stay a while? To have another beer? I hate going home this early. My parents'll still be up."

"You live with your parents?"

"For a year or so now." She paused, and her chest rose and fell with a long breath. "I was living with someone and he moved out. It was too much for me to make rent and a car payment on my own. So 'til I can save up, I get to live at home with my two darlin' little half-sisters and feel like the black sheep of the family." She absently rubbed a hand over the rose tattoo on her arm; it was a traditional design with bold colors and heavy shadows. "Got that when I was younger and a lot stupider," she said lightly when she noticed that his eyes had followed her hand.

"I'm still young and stupid." Jason pulled up his shirt sleeve to reveal a cross drawn to look like it had been carved from old stone, and behind that, crossed drumsticks wreathed in blue flames. Donna traced the cross with a fingertip, and he shrugged it back under his shirt.

"Yeah, I remember checkin' your I.D. for the first time and thinking that you were way too young and hot to be drinking all by yourself in a hole like Sam's. The beard makes you look a little older, though."

"Just trying out something different," he said, touching his darkly whiskered face.

"Something to hide behind?"

"I guess. I haven't wanted to be bothered. Not that many people would notice, or bother at any rate." Nedra had been the one people recognized. She stood out—she shone—or she had, anyway. An image of her flashed into his mind—his beautiful girl, his whole life, kneeling among glass shards and water spattered across the kitchen tile, and screaming at him as he tried to help her clean up the mess. Screaming at herself, really, but he was too close to know the difference. She had managed to cut the same finger that bore the ring he had given her, and when she had seen the blood, she had collapsed into a weeping mess and had not let him touch her. He picked his beer back up and emptied it.

Donna looked over her shoulder and considered the drum set on the other side of the room. "I wouldn't have pegged you for a Christian music fan. My sisters listen to that stuff."

He guessed that she had recognized the band name, Mercy Mercy, spelled out in gleaming silver on the front of the bass drum, but had not realized why the lettering would be there. "That stuff?" He let out a humorless chuckle. "A lot of it is pretty bad, to be honest, but I think we were alright. Sometimes I don't even know why I brought those damn drums with me, though."

Her eyes narrowed and then widened as she looked back at the drums and then at him. "You were in that band?" She took in his nod. "Wow, now I feel like an ass. Jesus."

"Yeah, Jesus and southern rock." He tried to keep equal measures of regret and bitterness from seeping into his voice. They had been on the verge of going somewhere—out of the Bible belt—maybe big time.

Donna toyed with her beer bottle. "I don't go to church anymore. But I don't mind the Jesus bit so much. I like that one where he told those old guys off when they wanted to throw rocks at that lady. Where was her asshole boyfriend, anyway?"

Jason didn't have an answer for that. Jesus was fine. It was the asshole boyfriends who screwed things up.

"You still play?"

"I practice 'cause it's a habit, but in here," he motioned toward the low ceiling and blank walls, "and without the rest of the band, it just seems like noise." He took a deep breath. God, he had tried so hard to be good enough. The drums—they had been the easy part.

Donna bit her bottom lip. Pensively, not seductively. Her uncertainty made him feel better. She said, "I didn't mean to bring up any of that old shit we said we weren't going to talk about. Let's shut up and drink another beer."

"Good idea." Jason got up and returned with two freshly opened bottles.

They sat side by side for a few minutes and drank in silence until Donna leaned over to him and said, her breath warm in his ear, "If you wanted to kiss me, not for any good reason, I mean, just for the hell of it, you know . . . I wouldn't mind."

"I don't want to take adv . . ."

"I'm a big girl. I can handle it."

He kissed her—one long, tender, tentative kiss that came to an end when she pulled away, kicked her feet up on the other end the couch and slid down to nestle under his arm. "You are a nice guy. I can tell."

"Maybe. Just don't expect much, okay?"

"I never expect much outta guys anyway . . . and especially not guys who are a decade younger than me. Damn, my sisters would probably have the hots for you. They're 17 and 19—little church youth group princesses." She wrinkled her nose. "Oh God, I think they saw your band in concert once over in

Greenville. Maybe I should introduce you. They'd freak." She sounded mildly horrified by the idea.

So was he. "Nah, that's okay. I like you and your shitty past. Makes me feel like I'm in good company."

"Well, in that case maybe I'll keep you company for a while."

Donna's visits became more frequent and then habitual. If it wasn't too late, she would stop in on the way home from work, and on her nights off she would come over and sometimes bring dinner in Tupperware containers since he subsisted on sandwiches and canned soup. He couldn't figure why she liked spending so much time at his place when all they did was drink a few beers, watch TV, and talk about work or other things that didn't really matter. Her life at home didn't sound that bad except for the typical annoyances of sharing a small house with four family members and her mom's spoiled pack of lapdogs. Sometimes she would make him laugh and sometimes he would kiss her, and while now and then it felt like she wanted more, mostly she didn't seem to mind whether he kissed her or not. He was glad of that, because the tug of war in his insides—temptation and memory, hope and despair—was bad enough already.

After a couple of months, they had fallen into such a comfortable routine that she no longer knocked; he left the door unlocked when he was at home and she came and went as she pleased. Then one Friday night she showed up later than normal, bursting through the door and walking quickly past him into the kitchen. The glow of the fridge light briefly illuminated the darkened doorway, and he heard a beer cap hit the linoleum and roll away as he came into the room behind her. She leaned against the counter and downed a third of the beer before taking a breath and running a hand over her face.

He flipped on the light and she winced. "What is it, Donna?"

She shook her head and took another drink, then put the bottle down.

Jason took her hands in his. "Your hands are shaking. What's wrong?"

"It's one of those things we said we wouldn't talk about." She was upset, maybe even frightened, so he put his arms around her and she clung him, pressing her face into his neck. He thought she was going to cry.

"Tell me, Donna. It's okay."

She was quiet for a while and then, with her face still hidden against his shoulder, she murmured, "I lied to you . . . about why I'm living with my family."

She didn't say anything else, so he finally asked, "What does that have to do with you being upset right now?"

"Ray is back in town and he showed up at the bar tonight."

"Ray?"

"I used to live with him . . . until he pushed me off our front porch and broke my arm. That was almost two years ago."

Jason took her by the shoulders and stepped back so that he could see her. "This guy showed up and hassled you?"

Donna nodded and looked at the floor between them. "He kept tryin' to talk to me at the bar, but I was ignoring him as much as I could. When I got off, he was standing outside by my car so that I couldn't get in. He was trying to make nice, apologizing about the accident all over again . . . of course he told everyone it was an accident, the bastard."

"Did you tell anyone that it wasn't?"

"My family suspected, but I figured that if I didn't say anything about it, I wouldn't have to hear about it either. My mama acts like she never did a thing wrong in her whole life, like she forgot that before she got married and got Jesus, she got me first—and it wasn't no virgin birth either." She stopped suddenly and her face flushed pink. "Anyway, I just wanted to get away from him. I moved back home and he kept calling me for a while, but then he got a job out of town and was gone."

"You didn't report it?"

"No. It would've been my word against his, same as always."

She glanced up at him, her eyes glistening and her brow pinched. He realized how tight—painfully tight—his grip on her shoulders had become. He let her go and fled from those eyes. He ended up on the porch, where he stood with his hands on the railing, looking down the sloped gravel drive toward the highway.

She spoke from the doorway behind him. "I had been in a couple of relationships with guys that I liked, but who decided that they didn't like me enough to stick around. When I met Ray, he seemed to really want me, you know, and it was nice at first . . ."

"You don't have to explain yourself," Jason interrupted without looking back at her, but she continued anyway.

"Things started to change when we moved in together. He got possessive and jealous . . . and he'd just take what he wanted and I let him because I thought I loved him. I still didn't realize what an asshole he was. But then I got pregnant. I didn't know if he'd be happy about it, but before I even told him about the baby, I lost it, real early. I was kinda relieved, as bad as that sounds, but then he found out 'cause I had to go to the hospital and have a D&C."

She paused and he could hear her inhale slowly, as if gathering the resolve to finish the story. He didn't want to hear it. He wanted to turn and punch the rough square beam that supported the roof of the porch. Maybe break a knuckle or two.

"He thought that I had done something to end it, and he got angry. That's when things really got bad. I didn't wanna be with him anymore, but if I resisted, he would . . ."

"He'd hit you, right?" Jason gripped the railing hard.

"He'd slap me around, threaten me. He was smart enough not to leave bruises."

"So you didn't tell anyone." It was more of a statement than a question, and Jason regretted the way it sounded, but there was no taking it back.

"No. But I decided to leave him. He tried to stop me, and that's when he got mad and pushed me over the porch railing. He took me to the emergency room, but I never went back home with him." Her voice had become hard.

Jason didn't respond. What could he say to that?

Eventually she walked up behind him, put her arms around his waist and leaned into him. When she spoke her voice was softer, almost a whisper. "Did your dad leave bruises?"

"Sometimes." He didn't ask how she knew, whether she had guessed or whether she had read it in some interview he had done with the band.

"Did you ever hit your girl?"

The quiet question was a sucker punch and the answer hissed out through his clenched teeth, forced out with his breath before he could stop it.

"No, but I wanted to. That's why I fucking left."

Donna hugged him tighter, her hands crossed over his chest. "You're a good guy, Jason. You're a good guy because you wanted to, but you didn't."

"It doesn't make any difference."

"It did for her."

"I wouldn't know." Jason said this and turned back toward her, tilting her face up with one hand so that he could see it clearly in the glow of the security light. "He didn't put his hands on you tonight, did he?"

"He tried to get me to kiss him, but some people walked out of the bar and I told him that I'd scream. He let me go and I got in my car and left."

"I'll be there to walk you out tomorrow."

Jason was there at the end of her next three shifts, but Ray only came in once and sat at a table with some other guys. Donna discretely pointed him out and Jason watched him from his usual spot at the far end of the bar. Seeing the man in person, he understood one reason why Donna said that she had let Ray take what he wanted. She couldn't have stopped him if she had tried. Ray was a big guy—tall, with tattooed arms that stretched the fabric of his Clemson Tigers t-shirt. He didn't hassle Donna, but he did watch her often as she moved up and down the bar, working and trying to ignore the fact that he was even in the building. Jason sat there until Ray and his friends left, and then checked the parking lot to make sure that they were gone before Donna's shift ended.

Two nights later, when she was scheduled to work again, Jason called the bar to catch her in the lull between the early dinner rush and the later drinking crowd. His old Bronco had broken down as he was leaving work, and he had had to give up on it until he could get to the auto parts store in the morning. He had caught a ride home, staring at the black grease smudges on his hands and jeans and thinking about her all the way. "Get someone to walk out with you, even if you haven't seen Ray around tonight. Just to be safe," he told her. She agreed in an offhand way so he persisted, "Promise me you will, or I'm gonna walk down there and do it myself. It's only two miles."

"Okay, I promise. I think Sam's staying to close tonight, so I'll wait on him. I gotta get back to work."

Jason said goodbye and hung up, satisfied. The bar didn't close until eleven, so he figured that she would go on home when her shift ended. He had already locked up for the night and had fallen asleep on the couch in front of the TV when her insistent knock startled him awake.

"Sorry, I didn't mean to wake you," Donna said as he let her in, "Ray showed up after all and sat at the bar for a couple of drinks. It kinda freaked me out because his truck was still in the parking lot when I left. Sam walked out with me, though, and I didn't see Ray. He must've left with one of his friends."

"It's okay. Are you alright?"

"Yeah, but I feel gross from gettin' ogled all night. I . . ."

She went quiet when the front windows lit up with the glare of headlights. Jason walked to the window and looked out at the truck that had pulled up in the shadows behind Donna's car.

"Shit. We got company," Donna whispered as if Ray might hear her from where he still sat in his truck. "He must've followed me."

Jason was pulling on the work boots that he had left lying by the door. "I'll take care of this." He yanked up the zippers on the inside of each boot and pulled his jeans back down over them.

Donna had cracked open the door and looked out.

Ray called to her from the driveway. "So you living in this little dump now?"

"Get outta here, Ray. I don't wanna talk to you."

"Come on, baby. Gimme a chance."

"Go away."

"How long you been living here? I thought you were still staying with your mama and stepdaddy."

Jason pulled Donna back, and she held onto him, a little wild eyed. "Don't," she said.

"Just stay inside," he told her, and pushed the door closed. He walked out and down the three porch steps to the ground, which was probably a mistake. Damn, Ray was tall. This wasn't Jason's his first go-round, though, and he wasn't a kid anymore. He gave Ray a hard look. "She doesn't live here. I do. And this is private property. You need to leave."

"Oh yeah?"

"Yeah. She doesn't want to talk to you, and I will call the police."

"Oooh," Ray mocked, "And what are you gonna do in the twenty minutes that it will take the slow ass podunk P.D. to get over here?"

"Whatever I need to."

"Tough guy, huh?" Ray strode toward him, but Jason stood his ground and Ray stopped only inches away, jerking his arms as if he were going to throw a punch.

Jason wasn't about to let the big man think that he was intimidated. He stood still and kept his clenched fists at his sides. "Get the fuck out of my yard."

"You gonna make me?"

Jason heard the door open behind him, and then Donna's voice. "Jason, don't . . ."

He opened his mouth to speak just as Ray's fist shot out with a vicious blow and then another that caught him center mass, right below the ribs, and drove all of the air out of his lungs. His vision blurred and he clutched his stomach with one hand as his knees buckled. "Shit," he gasped.

"You aren't even worth the time it would take to kick your ass." Ray chuckled and aimed a kick at him, but Jason was fast enough to raise both hands and block it, although the force rocked him back off of his knees. Ray was surprised but laughed it off, giving a dismissive wave and turning to walk back to his truck. "I'll let you off easy this time, buddy."

Jason felt his anger flare white hot, and for once he let it. It made him reckless. "You leave her alone or you'll regret it," he called, trying not to wince as he rose to his feet. "I don't care how big you are, you fuckin' piece of trash."

Ray turned back. "Oh, so you're a scrappy little guy, huh? Cute." He charged. Jason fended off the first few blows and managed to jab a fist into Ray's side, but it didn't have much effect. They tussled for a moment until Ray broke free and landed a jarring punch to Jason's left cheekbone with a big hand that sported some kind of school or signet ring. There was a bright starburst of pain, and Jason's head rang as Ray laughed again, taunting him as he stumbled to one knee.

"You better give it up while you can, you dumb little fuck." Ray turned to walk down the gravel drive toward his truck.

The pain in his diaphragm and his head were too familiar, and they only made Jason angrier. He squeezed his eyes shut for a moment and all his flaming rage, all his hot yellow shame coalesced like a target on that broad back. He took a deep breath and ran down the slope. Ray didn't have time to turn around before Jason jumped, hitting the big man's with his full weight and using the momentum to ride him to the ground. They fell hard, Ray face-first into the gravel with Jason on top of him. Jason moved fast, scrambling up and dropping back down hard, driving his knee twice into Ray's lower back, eliciting a grunt and then a loud groan of pain. Ray tried to get his arms under him to push up, but Jason gave him another vicious knee to the kidney and smacked his face into the gravel.

It wouldn't last long, but for the moment, Ray was too stunned by the pain to struggle. Jason knelt on his back, knees spread wide to make the most of his weight, and leaned down toward Ray's ear. "How much blood you wanna piss for the next few days, big guy?"

Ray grunted and spat, panting. "Get the hell off of me. I'll kill you, you little fucker!"

In the glow of the security light, a few of the whitish rocks stood out, darkened by blood.

"No, if I let you up, you're gonna get the hell out of here, and you aren't gonna bother Donna again, ever."

"You let me up and you better watch your fucking back." He tried again to get his hands under himself to push up and throw Jason off.

Jason punched the other side of Ray's lower back as hard as he could—he might not be big, but he was strong enough—and Ray quit struggling, his hands instinctively moving to try to protect his pummeled kidneys. Jason leaned forward again. "You don't understand, friend. You won't catch me off guard next time, and I don't have much going for me right now. So if you mess with Donna, I might just kill you. Little fucker or not." He thought he actually meant it, too, and it startled him. He inhaled sharply through his nose, trying to shake off the pain that radiated from his temple and cheek. "So what's it gonna be?"

"Okay. Whatever. Lemme up and I'll go."

"You better, Ray." It was Donna, who had come up behind them holding a longish, three-inch thick section of tree branch that she had pulled from the pile of firewood beside the cabin. She brandished it like a club. Jason jumped up and backed toward her, taking the makeshift weapon as Ray slowly got up, holding his lower back with one hand and wiping his nose with the back of the other.

Ray sneered at them but made no move to continue the fight. "You can have her. Plenty of other dumb bitches out there . . . younger and hotter ones, too." He spat on the ground and stared Jason down one more time.

Jason propped the piece of wood on his shoulder like a baseball bat. "Get outta here."

Ray gave them a mocking bow and got into his truck. When he was gone, Jason threw the firewood aside as Donna wrapped her arms around him and burst into tears. They stood there for several seconds, and then Jason pulled her back toward the cabin.

"Let's go inside." The adrenaline was subsiding, and the pain swelled. His head throbbed every time one of his feet hit the ground, so he went up the porch steps slowly, then went inside and sat down on the couch. Donna knelt in front of him, still crying.

"You're bleeding. I didn't want you to get hurt." She reached up to touch his face. He leaned away from her fingers and lifted a hand to feel the damage for himself. There was broken skin just below his temple—he sucked a little air between his teeth when he touched it—and there was the stickiness of smeared blood, but not too much.

"I'll be okay. There's some first aid stuff in the bathroom cabinet, and pain pills, too."

Donna got up and came back in a minute with a first aid kit in a small plastic box, a bottle of pills, and a glass of water. Jason shook out four of the ibuprofen tablets and swallowed them in one gulp, and then let Donna wipe the blood away from the small laceration on his cheek.

"It's not bad," she told him, "the cut anyway. But you're already bruising up."

"God, I feel like I got hit by a truck. He only got me twice, but that was enough."

"I'm so sorry. I can't believe you did that. How'd you know how to keep him down?"

Jason gave a bleak chuckle and regretted it as the pain in his head and stomach flared at the same time. He took a shallow breath and then explained in a whisper, "When you come up rough and you're the smallest in the bunch, you learn how to fight dirty. But damn, I haven't been hit like that in a long time." He carefully rested his head against the back of the couch and closed his eyes. At least the blood on the gravel hadn't been his this time. It could have been so easily, though. What a damn idiot.

Donna gently placed two small butterfly stitches on his cheek. "Are you sure you don't want me to take you to the E.R.? You might have a concussion." She took his hands in hers, still kneeling in front of him.

"Maybe . . . but I'll be okay when this headache eases off."

"You shouldn't go to sleep for a while just in case."

Jason squeezed her hands. "Stay here with me, okay?"

"Of course I'm gonna stay. That was the most amazing thing anyone has ever done for me. Thank you."

Without opening his eyes, Jason made a doubtful grimace. He wasn't proud of himself and he didn't want her gratitude. But at least this time, maybe he had made a difference, and the bruises would be worth it. Maybe he had done for her what he hadn't been able to do for his mother.

"I'm serious," Donna said. "He could have really hurt you . . . God, I hope he didn't." She pushed his shirt up to look at his stomach, gingerly touching the skin between his ribs and his navel. There was a smudge of tiny red pinpoints to mark the place where Ray's big ring had dug into his diaphragm, and that was probably just the beginning.

"Yeah, that'll be sore," he whispered, "But don't worry. It'll be okay. I'd do it again if I had to."

She pushed herself up and kissed him, then sank back between his knees and rested her face on his chest. Jason put his arms around her shoulders but kept his eyes closed.

The gentle pressure of Donna's fingers dabbing the blood off of his cheek and the sound of her quiet weeping had taken him back to another time, and to her. That night it had been the E.R. nurse who had dabbed away the blood and pressed the butterfly stitches into place above his eyebrow, but later, after paper shuffling and phone calls and questions about what to do with a seventeen-year-old boy who couldn't go back home, she had been there. The same sheriff's deputy that had found him walking down the two-lane toward town had taken him to her house, and when Nedra had run out to meet him in the yard, he had smiled even though it made his lip split open again. She had cried over the blood too, and he had been happy to bleed. That was the night she had become his home.

Homesickness rose up in him and he pressed his eyes shut against the tears that tried to well up with it, but the movement sent another shot of pain through his cheek and he let out a grunt of discomfort.

Donna shifted between his knees. "You should let me do something for you . . . something to help you feel better."

She sank a little lower and he felt her fingers slide along his stomach just above the waistband of his jeans. He opened his eyes and looked down at her for a second before it dawned on him what she meant. He sat up and then back again when his aching head protested the rapid movement. He reached down and pulled her up toward him. "Donna, you don't have to do anything for me. Not like that."

"I know, but I want to, and it's not like you'd be cheating on anyone. Endorphins are natural painkillers, you know." She pushed up his shirt and he felt her warm breath on his skin.

He caught her hand and held it still, and then he felt his face grow hot as he spoke. "I've never done that before."

Surprise registered in her eyes. "You're a virgin?"

"Uh, yeah, because of her, I was waiting." It was a half-truth at best. He had never done what he assumed Donna had in mind, but he didn't like to admit the truth. He had slept with the one girlfriend he had during that year he got sent to live with his grandparents, and damn, he thought, he had done that wishing she had been someone else too. He had barely been sixteen, and later it had been one more reason for him to feel like he didn't quite measure up.

"Don't take it the wrong way, okay . . . listen, I don't want to use you like that and then leave. I don't want another reason to feel like an asshole."

"You are not an asshole. Why won't you listen to me when I tell you that? If I want to do something for you—freely, with no strings attached—how does that make you the bad guy?"

"I don't know if I'll ever be able to go back home, but if I do, I don't want to go back feeling like I've fucked things up even more. I'm sorry. I can't get her out of my head. I've loved her since I was fifteen."

"I don't understand why you are fucking around here, then. If you love her so much, go do something about it. Get her back."

"It's not that simple."

"What could you have done that's so bad that you can't go back and at least try to fix it? Hell, you got mad and wanted to hit her? Who doesn't want to hit somebody every now and then? You didn't do it. You aren't this terrible person that you seem to think you are."

"It's not just that I wanted to hit her . . . it's that things weren't working, no matter what I did. There was this accident and she got hurt . . . but it was more than that. It messed with her head. She got, was, I guess . . . sick. I mean, depressed and moody, angry, sometimes out of control. She couldn't help it, but I couldn't handle it. I felt like I was turning into someone that I didn't want to be. Someone who was bad for her."

"Your father."

The tension that had crept into his body made him hurt, but he couldn't let it go. "Yeah, and she saw it too . . . she saw it and it killed me."

"But you made a choice not to be like him. And just now you made a choice to not be like the other guys who have used me and treated me like shit. If you keep choosing to be the good guy, you will be. For me, you already are."

Jason held her to his chest and tried to believe her, but the echoes of rage inside of him—the memories of the red outlines that his thumbs had pressed into her shoulders, and of the spittle he had sprayed with threats into Ray's ear—whispered to him other, truer things.

You can get kicked out or you can walk out, but some of the places you come from just won't leave you behind.

ABOUT THE AUTHOR

Dr. Leslie Maxwell Kaiura is an Associate Professor of Spanish at the University of Alabama in Huntsville. She teaches all levels of Spanish language, culture, and literature and is a member of the Women's and Gender Studies faculty. Her area of research focuses on gender ideology and violence against women in 19th and early 20th-century Spain, and she has published scholarly articles in journals and edited collections. She is an amateur theology nerd and dreams of one day publishing the novel from which the story "Company" originated.

WE THREE SPIES OF PARTHIA ARE

JAMES F. MCGRATH

The royal palace in Ctesiphon is breathtaking to behold, especially when seen in the dazzling sunlight of a clear spring day. The sheer height and length of its famous mudbrick arch seems to defy the pull of Earth, as though it were suspended from the heavens by an invisible cord. I have heard visitors say that the hand of Ahura Mazda holds it aloft from above, and I have heard unscrupulous tour guides claim that once, centuries ago, the great God had momentarily frozen the two great spirits in place as they wrestled for the souls of humanity, and that none other than Zarathustra himself had built the structure upon their backs. Such stories are recent fabrications, idle imaginings and nothing more. For those of us less inclined to think about a building in mythical terms, we are struck instead by the architectural skill that is on display, the genius that planned its construction and the skill of the workers who brought that vision to fruition. The arch proclaims to one and all the collective greatness of our kingdom and its people, our abilities that extend from feats of engineering and military prowess to astrology and art. Ultimately, I suppose it doesn't really matter which view of this marvel one prefers. Either God teaches our rulers and builders what he does not teach to people in other lands, or else the very hand or power of God supports the city's legendary archway, just as he supports the city itself which in turn governs and maintains the entire kingdom. Either way, it makes its impression and communicates its message. Once one finally lowers one's gaze from the breathtaking vault overhead, one is confronted with the painted reliefs that adorn the corridors of the palace, beginning from the grandiose entranceway. In vivid colors they tell the heroic and inspiring stories of the one God and his messengers, of our kings and the mighty heroes who have served them valiantly.

That is what one sees by day. A spy, however, is expected to arrive by cover of night, when the magnificent arch is transformed into a threatening scimitar, raised to strike down enemies, a dangerous cover that blocks the moon's light and veils the palace entrance in a shroud of darkness. The impression conveyed when one arrives at night has always seemed to me more appropriate. Friend and foe alike do well to approach with reverence and fear, since it was as perilous to visit a wrathful king as it was to stand beneath the flaming sword of a capricious deity. Beauty strikes awe into the heart, but it also extends a welcome. At night, however, the carved figures that adorn the walls are transformed from stunning narrations of inspiring stories to fleeting figures who are glimpsed only to disappear suddenly from view. When passing torchlight brings a painted figure into view, it seems to glare with suspicious eyes, its menacing gaze appearing to follow one's stealthy progression towards the royal throne room. There are also guards in the shadows, hidden from view in alcoves, but always alert. From these beings of flesh and blood like mine I have nothing to fear. Unlike the mythical heroes that adorn the walls, some of whom were known to have been capricious and unpredictable, most of the king's retinue knows my faithful service and that, if I and my fellows have been called to converge on this place at this hour, and the king awaits us, it is for a mission of the utmost importance. The soldiers do not move as we pass, and yet while the static gazes of the faces carved into the walls seem to follow us despite their being unable to do so, the living guardians of the palace do not budge in the slightest, yet we know our every move is carefully tracked and scrutinized by their unwavering eyes.

The throne room itself contains a far greater number of torches and other sources of light, to ensure that the king's plans, which often involve writing letters or outlining strategy on a wax tablet, can be prepared and enacted unhindered. Although we arrived separately, the three of us who now assembled before the throne knew one another well. Usually we worked separately, a lone individual being capable of far more stealth than any larger group. Sometimes our separate missions might overlap, and we would exchange the briefest of knowing glances as we spotted one another in a lonely street or crowded marketplace in a city in a foreign land. If we have been assembled together at one time in this way, it will surely be for a highly unusual mission, and thus a significant one.

"Our struggles against Herod are not proving as successful as they must!" boomed the voice of king Arsaces from his throne. His voice was a commanding one in its own right, and his family's royal pedigree, combined with his own successful reign thus far, lent further weight to all of his pronouncements. "His tiny kingdom would not stand against us, were it not for his alliance with Rome, and Rome would not behave so arrogantly towards us were Herod's kingdom not a buffer between us and them. A frontal military assault will only lead to extended war that would drain our resources. But I have a plan for how to undermine Herod by stealthier means."

We three spies stood at attention, transfixed. The king was a capable military strategist, and he had excellent advisors. He might call his spies to consult on a plan, but only after he had taken counsel with his wisest generals and magi about whatever the plan might be. Other kings must discuss matters of espionage in whispers behind locked doors, even within their own palaces. King Arsaces knew that he could trust every man present and had no need to fear that enemies would spread abroad the things spoken here, however deadly their secrets might be.

"How much do you know about the kingdom of Israel?" The king asked us.

We looked at one another. Israel was a longstanding enemy, ever since the region had been wrested from our control by the Greeks. Now it was in the hands of the Romans, for all intents and purposes, with yet another puppet king on the throne.

"We have learned a great deal about them and their ways, sire, as we have undertaken your missions there in the past," I answered. "What is it your pleasure to know about them? We will surely find it out for you, if we do not already know it."

The king looked amused at my cautious answer, deferring to him while also claiming competence, and as a result really saying nothing at all. "Do you know their superstitions?" the king asked me. "Do you know the history of their kings?"

It was Balthazar who answered before I managed to. "We know that the current king is not well liked, despite the prosperity that his reign has brought about," he said. "Some look back to a golden age when another family sat on the throne, and hope that the kingdom will one day be returned to those hands."

The king laughed heartily. "Very good! That is indeed the case. And that is the wedge that we shall use to split Herod's kingdom and splinter it."

"My lord," I said, "there may be descendants of that more ancient line of kings that still live. Shall we find them for you, so that you can support them against Herod?"

"Oh, we need not do anything as obvious or as crass as that," the king replied. "All that needs to happen is for Herod to *believe* that a king is emerging from elsewhere. We have seen his paranoia at work, and know that even his wives and children are not safe when he becomes suspicious. All we need to do is feed that suspicion, so that a cancerous distrust will grow within him. It will sap his strength and divide his mind as well as his family, and ultimately his kingdom."

The king proceeded to outline his plan to us. It was even more brilliant than I had expected. We were to go to Jerusalem – all three of us together – bearing gifts and claiming to be magi who have seen in the stars that a new king has been born who will rule over Israel. Herod will become distressed. His family and servants will whisper and plot. Their doom will emerge mostly from within, and then when Parthia knocks on the door, it may simply open to us, to settle the chaos that has been resulting from Herod's mania. But at the very least, Rome's border region will be unsettled and our own border will be more secure as a result. It was a brilliant plan, and as a strategist I felt rather ashamed to not have thought of something like it myself. I wondered which of the king's advisors had come up with it, or whether it was his own cunning that had devised it. Either way, the risks to the kingdom were few even if they should fail, although obviously if Herod saw through the plan, our own individual lives and those of anyone else on the mission with us would be forfeit. And the reward should they succeed was almost unfathomable.

The king provided us with lavish clothing of the sort the most esteemed and influential of the magi wear. He also provided us with gold, frankincense, and myrrh to bring as gifts. And of course, travel papers. As spies we were used to traveling to Judaea via the more direct and dangerous caravan route that runs through the desert. It follows a gorge that spans almost the entire distance of the journey, and which flows with water during the rainy season. We can usually take that most of the way, veering off only a half a day's journey or so before we reach the border, in order to avoid the outpost situated at the point at which the route crosses from Parthian territory into that of Rome's vassal. Not this time. This time the whole point of our journey is that we be seen, that we make our entry into Jerusalem a cause of commotion. It made for a welcome change, to be honest. I rarely had the opportunity to travel in such luxury. Seldom did my role as spy involve impersonating or pretending to be a dignitary or someone of means. While the king ensured that I was well-paid and had ample funds for any mission I went on, the travel itself usually involved neglected byways, desert detours, and wading through unpatrolled segments of rivers under cover of night. Now I was making my way by camel, with a retinue of a sufficient number of the king's servants acting as my own so as to make my false identity and that of my two colleagues seem plausible to all whom we encounter – including, most crucially, Herod himself.

Our route took us northwards along the Euphrates via Dura Europos. The changes in climate as well as in political realities were noticeable as we drew near to the border crossing into Roman Syria. When the Roman soldiers asked our business, we answered honestly: we have come to honor the king in Jerusalem, bringing gifts of tribute from the East. The soldiers viewed us with some suspicion, looking closely at out papers. Having searched us for weapons and found none other than what one would expect servants of dignitaries to carry in order to defend them from robbers on the road, we were allowed to pass – but only with an escort, which would ensure that we journeyed on safely to Herod's palace in Jerusalem. Two soldiers from the cohort accompanied us as far as Panias in the northern part of Herod's Kingdom. They made a point of steering our route so that we got a good look at the Augusteum that Herod had built there in honor of the emperor and gods of Rome. I would happily show them Ctesiphon and see if they could remain so misguidedly proud! But such architectural propaganda abounds in every kingdom, and I knew it was my duty to gaze at it with feigned awe, resisting the strong temptation to sneer contemptuously. From there, we would be taken by soldiers belonging to Herod's vassal kingdom. The way this all unfolded was a real godsend as far as our mission was concerned. Even if we had made it no further than this point, word would spread of our arrival up the Roman chain of command. Why would the Parthians be communicating with Herod and sending gifts to him? To lure him away from faithful allegiance to Rome? Might they be successful? Herod was bound to find himself under close scrutiny as a result of our arrival alone, whatever else might transpire in the remainder of our journey.

Although the Greek spoken by the Roman soldiers had been intelligible, the Aramaic of Herod's men, despite their accent, was much easier to understand. Neither language was as beautiful or logical as Persian, but the Babylonian language and writing system remains in wide use even today in much of our empire, much as is true of Greek in most of the eastern part of Rome's empire. The Herodian escort was of real benefit to our mission, just as the Roman one had been. As we proceeded southwards towards Jerusalem, their presence conveyed the impression to all who saw us that this was indeed a delegation of emissaries from Parthia to the king. What could this mean? Would fighting take place again between the Romans and the Parthians, with Israel caught in between? Would Herod switch sides? Should the people entrust their fate to Herod or express loyalty directly to Rome, so that any Roman displeasure that might ensue would be taken out only on Herod and not on them? Far from seeking to remain silent in the face of questions or dismissing inquiries from passersby as inappropriate, Herod's men spoke and speculated openly with people they met in various towns we passed through along our way, most of whom we gathered were previously known to our escorts.

Jerusalem did not come into view fully until we were surprisingly close to it. While other citadels sit on the highest hilltop anywhere in sight, visible from miles away, the topography seemed to obscure Jerusalem so that we first caught fleeting glimpses of it, as though the city were aware of our plan and taunting us, daring us to find it. And then suddenly it was upon us, as though it had crept up on us like an enemy, to leap out and subdue us before we could ready ourselves in defense. Even with having been to the city before more than once, the effect of its location in relation to the landscape remained disconcerting.

When at last we reached the city walls, we proceeded through one of the gates that led to a relatively straight street, full of sellers of goods ranging from fruits and vegetables to wooden tools and utensils. The temple and Herod's palace towered above all other structures, on opposite ends of the city, proclaiming to all that Herod believed himself to bear an authority like that of a god, or perhaps, the authority of his god. Our course towards the king's abode was guided by the tall towers of the palace, much as we would tell others that our journey to Jerusalem had been guided by a bright star. Once we entered the palace, we were asked to wait in a lavish antechamber where attendants washed our feet, provided food and drink, and made us comfortable. Others who had arrived before us to seek an audience with the king were already there in that room, and so we anticipated that we might have to wait for some time. It was not long at all, however, before the king's servant re-entered the room, his brow crinkled with evident concern, and told us that the king wished to speak to us next.

Herod's throne room conveyed as much about him as the palace's elevation, towers, and other aspects of its external appearance did. Everyone has heard stories of Herod's fortress at Masada, which has enabled him to weather challenges to his power. It is impenetrable in every meaningful sense of the word. Believe me, I know someone who tried to infiltrate it. Knew someone, that is. Perhaps precisely because of its inaccessibility, perched atop sheer cliffs near the Dead Sea, members of Herod's retinue seemed to feel no need to keep secrets about what could be found inside. Enormous cisterns of water. An ornately decorated hot bath and steam room. Of course, they could all he made-up stories, propaganda intended to impress and mislead. But such stories had reached me from multiple sources, and they had always struck me as believable, even before I had entered Herod's palace here in Jerusalem and seen the same combination of fortification and luxury. The ornamental frescoes matched the descriptions I had heard about Masada. And set into the ornate walls were alcoves in which soldiers could be glimpsed in the shadows, ready to respond at a moment's notice. If spies penetrated into the king's presence through deceit as we had, and sought to seize the opportunity to attack him with concealed weapons, they would be dead before they reached the first step leading up to the elevated platform where Herod's throne stood. The platform itself offered some protection, putting the would-be attacker at a disadvantage, while elevating the king in much in the same way the raised platform situated the palace itself above the city. My lord, the king of Parthia, was wise to assign us a different sort of mission than that.

"I am told that you have come with gifts for me!" Herod bellowed from his throne. His voice was higher pitched than I would have imagined, given his stocky build, a result of his life experience combining battle experience in earlier years and opulent self-indulgence more recently. Yet the resonant echo in the large hall added depth and richness to the voice. Such expansive throne rooms are typical in any palace across a wide array of different kingdoms. And yet one got the distinct impression that Herod might have thought consciously about the space, about how his voice sounded in it, about the need to convey a commanding presence that elicited awe and obedience on an instinctive level even from those who entered with hostile intent or indifference. My throat felt drier than I would have liked, and seeing my hesitation Melchior spoke courageously the words that had been scripted for us, rehearsed for this moment.

"Your majesty, I fear there may have been a misunderstanding," Melchior said. "We respect your greatness and pay you tribute. But our mission was in response to the sign that we saw in the sky, a star that we recognize as heralding the birth of a new king. We assumed that you had had a son born to one of your wives…"

The whispers among the attendants began almost immediately. They were as discreet as they could be, since even the quietest speech carried further than one might wish in that echoing chamber. I expected the king to become enraged and demand silence, but he simply turned an angry gaze around the room and all chatter quickly ceased. From the shadows, I saw a man step forward whom I soon recognized as Antipater, Herod's son, as soon as he drew near enough to the torch on the nearby wall, which had until this point enabled him to remain hidden in the shadow cast by the closest pillar to it. Antipater was Herod's firstborn, but his status as heir was not a given. He and his mother had been exiled when Herod took another wife, and so the possibility that his father had another son who might supplant him would unsettle him. I was glad that the words Melchior uttered were heard by Antipater with his own ears, rather than having to reach him as gossip and hearsay, even though even mere rumors about this would be certain to unsettle him. We must proceed cautiously. Our lives might already be forfeit. But if we have planted just the right seeds of discord, we might escape with our lives, as well as leaving the land of Judaea in turmoil.

Herod's eyes locked with Antipater's for the briefest of moments, then he gestured towards him as he returned his gaze towards us and addressed us. "My son is here, but this is a very belated present for his birthday, if that is what you intended."

"Your majesty," I began, feeling that I must take the lead in, and the responsibility for, what happened next. "If it is your wish, we shall present him the gifts we have brought. However, that is not our mission, and our lord the king of Parthia shall be displeased with us. The star's appearance leaves us in no doubt as to its significance. It signals that a king has been born at the time of its rising."

"When did that occur?" Herod asked us.

"Almost two years ago," Balthazar responded. We had determined that was a good time frame, not so recent as to sound implausible, but not far enough in the past that it could denote one of Herod's own sons. Herod motioned to one of his attendants to approach, whom he then commanded to run some errand. We waited for several minutes in awkward silence, before the arrival of several men who carried scrolls and appeared to be scholars.

"Scribes, I have a question for you about the Law. I know the answer, but I seek your confirmation. Where will the anointed one, the son of David, be born?"

The scribes looked at one another nervously, not because they did not know the answer immediately, but because they feared this was somehow a trick question, a test of their loyalty.

"In Bethlehem, sire," one of the scribes said, finally finding his voice.

"Very good," Herod said. "We can send these visitors forth to deliver their gifts there. Then they shall return to me and tell whether they found the newborn king they are seeking. After they do, they must return here with details of where he is located, so that I too may pay him homage."

Bethlehem? This was most unexpected. I vaguely knew the place, had heard tell of it, might have passed that way without stopping while on some mission. It was a small town, uninteresting and unimportant. Were we really to journey there? Was this a ruse on Herod's part? If we headed back to Parthia now, Herod would be able to discern that we had been insincere, willing to leave our purported mission unfulfilled. We must go to Bethlehem. But what should we do once we get there? We can find a home in which there is a young child, pay him homage, and then bring Herod word – or perhaps depart thence for Parthia, lucky to escape with our lives?

The journey from Jerusalem to Bethlehem was not a long one. It took us only a couple of hours to reach the small town. Our approach caused quite a stir, as no dignitaries had any reason to visit such a place. Yet here we were, three foreigners with an entourage, heading towards the tiny town, thoroughly unexpected. They had every right to be suspicious, to run to and fro as they spotted us in the distance, to shelter their women and station a select group of men to meet us at the edge of the habitation. We were so very clearly out of place. Was this why Herod had sent us here, to humiliate us? Was he laughing as he sent us on a fool's errand, having seen through our ruse? No, Herod might appreciate comedy, but he was not so merciful. He surely had people in Bethlehem who were loyal to him, and this too was a concern for us. We had seen no one on the road behind us whom we believed to be following us, but it was a road with a fair amount of foot traffic throughout the day and so we could not be sure. Whether it be among those who awaited us or those who would come after, or indeed both, there were surely some who would bring Herod a report. If they had not been sent expressly by him on such a mission, they would still run to tell what they had seen in exchange for a small sum of money, or in exchange for their lives being spared if they were threatened. We would have to play our parts until the end of this show, even as the script seemed increasingly bizarre.

"Welcome, honored guests!" said a man who stood in the road with a number of other townspeople, blocking our tiny caravan from proceeding further even as he extended his greeting. He spoke Aramaic with the distinctive lilt of Judaea, pleasant to listen to and easy to understand even for those who interacted mostly with speakers in Syria or the Babylonian heartland. "What is your business in Bethlehem?" he continued. "How may we assist you?" A wise and diplomatic individual if ever there was one. And a brave one, too. No breach of hospitality, yet using the very act of welcome to find out what he could, all the while standing between us and the neighbors and friends that he wished to protect. A man worthy of our respect, even as we continue our charade.

"We have come seeking a child who was born here, no more than two years before now," Balthazar said to him, our Parthian accents noticeable, not that anyone seeing our clothing would not already know that we had come from some such faraway place. "We have seen a sign that a king has been born in the land of Israel," I added, "and we have come to honor him."

The stirring and anxiety in the group of men was palpable. They had already been made uneasy by our approach. Now they could well have panicked. Their spokesman, however, took counsel with them. While the birth of children in a town this size would be common knowledge, there could be many or few, and it would be easy to neglect to mention someone. But what would the implications be of telling us what we wanted to know? Once again the man showed himself to be remarkably shrewd. He could legitimately give the appearance of merely trying to provide the information we requested, even as he discussed what they should do in this unusual circumstance. If the opportunity arises, I will recruit this man to serve as my informant here.

"There are too many families with children in the town that age for us to know whom you are referring to," he eventually replied. "But there is one family that hosts strangers from out of town, who came here around the time you mentioned, and are still here. The woman was already expecting a child when she arrived, and gave birth soon after. Perhaps they are the ones you are looking for?"

A wise man indeed. Sacrifice the stranger, the newcomer in their midst, if there is to be trouble. And well he might be concerned. I had been so determined to play my role in this ruse faithfully, to serve my king and harm his enemies, that I had not thought until now about the implications for innocents who might get caught up in it. What will happen to this little town of Bethlehem, to the family and child that shall soon become the recipients of our gifts? Will Herod seek them out? Will they be slaughtered? Despite having carried out assassinations often, I still felt sickened to my stomach at the thought that I might cost a young child and his hapless innocent family their lives. Whole villages could be burned, children massacred, women raped as an army moved through an area in a time of war. I had always thought of the role of a spy as being to prevent such things, offering targeted assaults that avoided innocent victims to the extent that international intrigue ever could. The way of espionage and assassination is much more humane and moral than outright war. But what of this plan that has led us in an unexpected direction? What will the cost be to these townspeople? A shiver ran up my spine, even though the early evening air was warm and dry.

We nodded our thanks to the townsfolk for their assistance, and made our way to the house they had referred to. We called out a greeting and waited only briefly before trying the door to see if anyone was inside. Within, in the lower chamber of the home, animals belonging to the family had already been brought inside for the evening – a number of goats, a couple of sheep, and two donkeys. In their midst, two young boys were playing. They both looked to be around two years old, although one might perhaps be slightly older than the other. On the raised main floor of the home, two women sat sewing, watching the children. From where they sat, they would have been unable to hear our call of greeting over the sounds in the home. But they saw us now that the door was open, and I watched as fear gripped them. They hesitated, conflicted whether to rush forward in an attempt to grab the children, or to run directly to another room or the courtyard where their husbands were to be found. I spoke quickly to try to defuse the situation and set their minds at rest.

"Fear not! We apologize for startling you. We mean you no harm. We have come on a mission of glad tidings and celebration. Please, are your husbands at home?" The two women hesitated, then one arose and, having made sure her companion was keeping her gaze fixed on us, moved cautiously to the rear door and looked out. After a few moments she shouted, "Zechariah! Joseph! Come quickly!" Looking out for a few moments longer, she returned to face us. We made no move to enter, knowing it would be improper to do so before the men arrived. This respect for propriety on our part seemed to relax the women significantly. The two husbands appeared in the rear doorway soon, clearly having been interrupted in the middle of some strenuous task, sweat still glistening on their brows.

Melchior spoke this time as we began to play out our script once more. "We bring you greetings from our brethren, the guild of astrologers in the East." Melchior wisely didn't specify that we had come from Parthia, knowing that mentioning this detail might frighten them and cause them to chase us away immediately. Any of Herod's subjects would naturally fear being reported as traitors merely for receiving Parthian guests.

"What has your astrology to do with us?" one of the men asked. He was stocky, and seemed rougher in both appearance and temperament than the other, whose robe seemed slightly finer and less worn, although both their faces reflected some way of life that took them in and out of the sun. They were neither as dark-skinned as shepherds and farmers nor as fair as princes.

Balthazar answered the question. "We saw a sign in the sky, a star giving indication that a new king had been born. It led us here. We come bearing gifts: gold, frankincense, and myrrh. Tell us please, which of you is the master of this house, and whose are the children?"

The two men looked at one another, nodded, and then the man who had spoken first moved forward towards the guests. "Our apologies for keeping you standing in the doorway. We expected no guests. Mary, Elizabeth, kindly bring some food." These last words were addressed to the women, who moved to set about the task immediately. As they disappeared out into the courtyard, the same man motioned our entire party to come into the house. Melchior asked if the servants might not take the animals to the town well to give them water first. The second of the two husbands came to the front door and, stepping outside, explained to our servants the way to the well. By the time he had come back inside, Balthazar, Melchior, and I were being seated in the house's main room by the man who now told us that his name was Joseph.

"You asked which of us is the master of the house, and that is a complicated question," Joseph explained. "It is my family home, but I have not been living here. I had moved up north temporarily, to work as a mason in building projects in Sepphoris in Galilee. There, I met the woman who would become my wife, and so I was in no hurry to return here. Meanwhile, my wife's cousin married a priest, Zechariah, and this house in Bethlehem was closer to Jerusalem than where they had been living. So they moved in. And then there was a census to register property owners, and so I needed to return here to maintain my claim to the land. As you can see, we are still here. Nonetheless, at the moment, my wife and I are in this house as guests."

"Don't be ridiculous, Joseph," Zechariah interjected. "This is your home."

"It is *our* home, for the moment," Joseph replied. "Both our families. All of us."

"And the children are yours?" I asked.

"We each have one son here. Mine is called Joshua. His is called John." He motioned with his hand in the direction of each of the boys in turn as he mentioned their names. Both of the children had already stopped their playing to stare with intense curiosity at the strangers that had appeared in their midst. Neither seemed inclined to come closer, despite their evident interest.

I could tell now that they must indeed be quite close in age. Which of them would be the one that ended up drawn into this increasingly complicated ruse? And what effect might it have on the boy?

"Which of them is the eldest?" I asked, hoping that might make what came next somewhat simpler.

"They are close in age to one another, as you can see," Zechariah replied. "John is older, but only by a few months. But – did you say you believe that a new *king* is in our midst? Surely you cannot mean one of our boys?"

"We believe that to be so," Balthazar told them. "The stars do not lie. We were led here to this place, by a star whose ascent we traced starting about two years ago. Would that not coincide with the time that your children were born?"

"Can you tell us the day that the star appeared?" Joseph asked. I quickly interjected, "We can, but we have no reason to believe that the star marked the very day of the new king's birth. Would that it were so simple! The stars do not communicate that way. The star will have ascended before him, announcing his appearance soon to follow." Melchior's puzzled glance in my direction only lasted a moment, then I saw his expression brighten as he realized I had avoided what could have been an awkward moment. If we offered a date that did not correspond to that of one of the boys' births, the fathers might have concluded that we were in the wrong place and sent us on our way, lengthening our quest.

"Then how are we to know which of the boys is the one you seek?" Zechariah asked us.

"That is for you to deduce, as the stars may guide you. We were led here to you. We will bestow our gifts on this home and those who dwell in it. The rest is up to you."

The two women had returned from the courtyard with bread, olives, and salt, which they set in our midst. It was unlikely either of them had overheard much if anything of our conversation thus far. Joseph stopped the two women before they could retreat back to the courtyard, and recounted to them what we had shared with them thus far. Both women looked astonished, as they stared first at us, then at one another, then at their children, then at their husbands. Soon all four of the adults of the house were engaged in a debate, insisting that one or the other of the boys was more likely to be the one we should honor. None of them seemed to be taking the matter all that seriously, and each seemed determined to conclude that it was the child that was not their own that we sought. Joseph emphasized that John was slightly older, while Zechariah reminded Joseph that his ancestors supposedly included none other than king David himself. While that detail made my heart race with excitement, Joseph brushed the suggestion aside dismissively. "So many people tell stories of their illustrious ancestors. How many of them do you think are true? I know several families that also say they come from the line of David, yet none of them claims to be related to me!"

The three of us who were guests ate mostly in silence as our hosts did most of the talking, continuing in this same manner. When the servants returned, we seized the moment of interruption to present our gifts to the two families. At this, they fell silent and the mood turned sober. Perhaps they had not taken the matter entirely seriously until the gold and other valuable items were set before them. While these families did not appear to be nearly as poor as the majority of people living in the town, they were clearly not used to seeing anything like such riches as those we had brought, never mind receiving them as gifts.

Norms of hospitality required them to offer us shelter for the night, and it was indeed getting late. Yet I felt we must refuse, in the interest of our own safety as well as theirs. Had anyone followed us? Would Herod's troops surround the home before morning and kill all inside? Would the townspeople already be gossiping to such an extent that even without spies or soldiers making inquiries, our words and actions here would be known in Jerusalem within a matter of hours? I had been surrounded more than once in my life by enemy soldiers determined to kill me, and yet I had never before felt such an urgent need to flee as I did now. As my eyes met those of the children, still watching us intently, I felt deep sorrow at the thought that I may have ended their lives prematurely by coming here into their home. I had thought Arsaces' plan brilliant, an inexpensive one that promised to bring so much benefit to Parthia. But it now seemed that the cost might be far greater than I envisaged. I realized, however, that I might be able to save their lives, without undermining the plan's aim.

"Alas, we cannot stay," I said to them. "We are expected back in Jerusalem before nightfall, and even if we leave now, I fear that darkness shall catch us before we arrive. But we dare not keep King Herod waiting." I had chosen my words carefully, and I could see that they were having the desired effect. As I had anticipated, Joseph and Zechariah looked nervously at one another, then at their wives and children. "Herod knows that you have come here?" Joseph asked us.

"He practically sent us. We arrived in Jerusalem first, since we expected to find a newborn king there, as I am sure you can understand. He told us to come to Bethlehem, expressing an eagerness to receive a report from us once we found this king, so that he too might offer his homage." I did not attempt to conceal the irony in my voice. If Herod came looking for a child that might ascend to the throne, his 'gift' for the child would be a sword, raised to strike a fatal blow, indeed to mercilessly hack the helpless infant to pieces in a horrifying fashion. Herod was well-known not only for his lavish tastes and his architectural achievements, but for the merciless cruelty with which he dealt with anyone who dared to cross him. I could see that all the adults present understood the warning that I was subtly delivering. What was being left unsaid up until that point now began to be spoken plainly.

"We cannot set out on a journey tonight," Zechariah said. "It is too late to be on the road with women and children. If we tried to reach even a city as near as Jericho, our bodies would be found along the road tomorrow, robbed and slaughtered."

"If we do not return tonight to Jerusalem, Herod may be suspicious, but will consider the possibility that we accepted your hospitality, or were delayed, or are in fact ourselves setting a trap of some sort for him. He will not rush to send troops here before morning. If you leave at the first light of dawn you will not have much of a head start, but I hope it will be enough. We will set out tonight towards the Jordan River. You should follow after us as soon as you can. You will eventually catch up with us on the way if we travel slowly once we are safely out of Herod's domain. You can seek refuge with us in Parthia. Those whom Herod despises and considers a threat will be welcome among us."

"No, I do not think fleeing to Parthia is the answer," Joseph opined. "There are Jews throughout Babylonia, to be sure, and we could settle amongst our scattered people there. But I have known many who have left the land of Israel for there, and few who have returned. Our home is here, and if we must flee, it will be to a place from which we can return as soon as the danger has passed."

"It is better for our party that we not return to Jerusalem at all," agreed Balthazar, not giving away to those who did not already know it the true nature of our mission here in Herod's land. But he made his meaning clear to us. "Herod would most likely simply kill us, after tormenting us and our servants to find out where we had been and whom we had visited. He would then seek you out and kill you here, if you remained, and would consider the matter concluded. That is not good for any of us. If you cannot travel with us tonight, we could wait for you somewhere beyond the Jordan. If you are still certain that you will not proceed with us back to Ctesiphon, so be it. We can depart thence, while you can take the King's Highway south towards Egypt and safety there. The trade routes between Egypt and your home are much more frequently traveled and are well maintained. It would be a safer and faster journey for you, with your women and children and whatever belongings you think you can take with you."

Joseph frowned, thinking deeply. "Egypt? Yes, there are many Jews there as well, and we could surely find a community that would receive us. But you should not wait for us. We will not join you to travel together as far as the King's Highway, to part ways there. There is no reason to slow your own journey and put yourselves at risk. We have another option. If we flee, Herod will expect us to journey together towards the east. Our presence would slow you down. We do not have horses or camels of our own, and you do not have enough for us. All our lives might be forfeit if you keep pace with us traveling on foot. I cannot bring this upon you if it can be avoided. There is another way. You travel that way on your own. If Herod does pursue you and catch you, you can say that you were frightened to return to him because you realized that the king you sought at first in Herod's court was in fact one he would perceive as a rival, and you were certain this would have made him angry. He might accept this excuse and allow you to leave unharmed. Meanwhile, we can travel towards the coast on country roads. I have done this once or twice before. These byways will not cause us to cross paths with soldiers from Jerusalem traveling via the main roads. We will eventually reach the Via Maris, which will take us to Egypt, and will do so more directly than the King's Highway. Even if Herod's troops realize that we have done this after first pursuing us eastward, even with their horses and their superior speed, they will be unlikely to overtake us before we make it to safety."

All of us looked at him, wondering what inspiration might have seized him, for him to have come up with this solution. It seemed far superior to what we, experts in stealth and subterfuge, had proposed. It was indeed a worthy plan, and we told him so, without revealing that it was the insight of long careers spent as spies that gave us this assurance. We attributed it to the stars, and before we left, I discreetly pointed to one that I told him would guide him towards the coast and the road to Egypt. It would indeed do this, but so equally would any other in that general direction. He did not need the star to find his way, but it seemed fitting to play our roles as astrologers to the end.

We set out towards our own land, the townspeople of Bethlehem still watching us with suspicion as we left. They could see that we were not returning by the route that had brought us into town. What would they make of this? Would any of them feel loyalty towards Herod and rush to send word? It would not matter. Once we were out of sight of the town we could quicken our pace, dropping all pretense of being foreign dignitaries. If we felt the need, we could steal some local clothing, separate from one another, and blend in among other travelers. But that shouldn't be necessary. We had an ample head start. This was as good a conclusion to our mission as we could have dared to hope for. Herod had been unsettled, and talk of this would spread in his family, and of course among his retainers and servants. From there it would leak into the general populace, and undoubtedly reach his enemies. With luck, he would not even know to seek the families of Joseph and Zechariah, but if he did discover which home we had visited, his men would hopefully find it empty. Even if he managed to kill them, niggling doubts would continue to plague him. And to top it all off, we had escaped with our lives. If we can make it to the crossing into Parthia, we will be safe, and once we reach Ctesiphon, we will be received with honor for having exceeded all expectations that any – even our lord the king – could reasonably have had when we set out. The undertaking had been brilliant, but it had also been risky, and whatever happened next in Israel after our departure, it would have been worth it for the trouble it brought upon Rome and its allies.

As it happened, at no point in our journey did we ever catch sight of troops pursuing us on the road. The journey back was so uneventful that it is hard to think of it as the epilogue to such a tale as ours. Truth be told, this was often how it felt when a mission of espionage concluded successfully. It was profoundly anticlimactic. It was the inept spy or assassin who barely escaped by the skin of their teeth. Their mission might have been accomplished, but at the cost of becoming known to their enemies and pursued by them. However odd the diminishing anxiety always felt after the suspense and danger that preceded, it was a testament to our skill at our profession.

We were indeed congratulated on our mission, once we reached the palace and gave our report to the king. It took some time for additional details to reach us about events that unfolded in Israel after we left, but which we could confidently attribute to results of our actions there. Herod had indeed sent troops to Bethlehem, and slaughtered every child born in the time period after we had said the star appeared. It was tragic, to be sure, but there were bound to have been only a tiny handful of children that age in so small a town. With any luck, the two of them we had met, John and Joshua, had escaped to safety. The number of Parthian children who died any time battles were fought with the Romans was always greater than the entire population of Bethlehem's children could have been. For the briefest of moments, I nonetheless felt a pang of guilt as I thought of the children I had glimpsed in the village, eyeing us with the same curiosity on the streets as young John and Joshua had when they were in their home. As I thought of the tiny infants that must have been needlessly torn from their mothers' arms and slaughtered. But I reassured myself that it was worth it. The spy's surgical approach, even in unusual cases like this one, was still more humane than full-scale war.

Later that same year, the news reached us that Herod's son Antipater had been executed. According to the report we heard, Varus, the Roman general who was now governing Syria, had Antipater brought before him, his loyalty to his father and to Rome having been called into question. I was curious enough that I sent word to my informants in Syria to find out more. As we suspected, Antipater had taken our talk of a sign as possibly referring to himself, heralding him as destined to ascend to the throne ahead of the expected time. He had been certain that, at the very least, the star had been a portent of doom for his father, and he was sure that his father's troops' atrocities in Bethlehem would cost him the loyalty of the people. He had thus plotted against him, hoping that whatever the correct interpretation of the sign in the heavens, his actions might appease the fates and secure his transition to the throne. His father Herod, however, had gotten wind of this. Why did he not just slaughter him on the spot? Why hand him over to the Romans? Clearly Herod was feeling hemmed in and constrained by both circumstances and Roman authority, while the Romans were at the same time losing their confidence in him. Our plan was working!

It was nearly two years later when Herod finally died. By then, I had been sent on another mission, to Armenia. That was another territory where Rome and Parthia each sought control, an uneasy truce on the surface hiding intrigue and subterfuge involving agents like myself. I managed to stay abreast of the story in Israel as it continued to unfold. Herod's son Archelaus ascended the throne after his father's death, but the people were unhappy. The Romans deposed him, and put down a popular rebellion that took place in response. Eventually they transferred Judaea to direct Roman rule, apportioning other fragments of Herod's kingdom among his sons. What a success! What had been cohesive was now divided, and where there had once been a buffer, now the domain of Rome itself lay right at Parthia's doorstep. There was no need to be a strategist like myself to easily see that this meant Rome's grip was weakening.

The struggle with the Romans continued throughout the remainder of my life. When I could no longer serve usefully as an active agent for my lord Arsaces, I asked for permission to remain in Armenia as an informant. I had rarely had the chance to spend a long time in one place since I had first entered the king's service as a soldier, when I was barely a grown man. No other place felt like home, and none provided me with a compelling rationale to return. If I relocated to Ctesiphon or Nisa, I would be an outsider, however much my reputation had remained known due to all my faithful service and accomplishments. Plus, there was squabbling over the throne, and I could easily find myself allied wrongly and wind up executed. Here I could simply be a distant but loyal servant of whoever happened to be on the throne, neither entangled in nor endangered by court intrigue.

Yet life beyond the most active forms of service to the empire left me with too much time to think. I had never married, and while the freedom had seemed welcome in my youth, now when companionship was a greater desire than sex, loneliness found me. So too did some guilt for things I had done. I still justified my actions as for the greater good. But when I slept, I sometimes dreamt of Bethlehem. At other times, I could not sleep because of my thoughts about it. When one is hungry for forgiveness, one may clutch at any offer. But I was not really like that. Other spies drank themselves into a stupor in their old age, as much from boredom as from guilt, I suspect. I still believed in what I had done. If I mourned the deaths of children in Bethlehem, my biggest regret was that I had not brought a fuller victory to my people. The struggle with Rome continued.

It was thus not because of any conscious religious longing that I opened the door to strangers who called out to me from the street. It was because, from their accents, they seemed to be Greeks from somewhere in the eastern provinces of Rome's empire, from someplace I knew I had been but couldn't quite place. Asia Minor, perhaps? They could be Roman agents, or ordinary folk with useful information that I could send back to my king. It was certainly worth my time to hear what they had to say. They said they had come to Aramosata bringing glad tidings. This introduction was odd, and yet they stirred my memories. This must have been how we sounded when we showed up in Herod's court all those years ago. Amused and intrigued, I indicated my willingness to listen, even though I perceived that these were peddlers of some sort of religious philosophy, the kind of thing that seemed more and more common these days. They said that the story they came to share could change my life, bringing me forgiveness and peace. I was unimpressed. However, when they said their message was about Israel's anointed one, my eyes grew wide and I stared at them incredulously. My curiosity was definitely piqued, but then my thoughts took an unsettling turn. This could not be a coincidence, surely! Perhaps they were Roman agents after all. I excused myself on the pretense of bringing them food, and while out of their sight, strapped my dagger to my leg. Had they managed to get the truth about our mission from someone who had been in our party? Who else knew the details, and might have divulged them? If they were here to mock me, they were surely also here to kill me. There are two of them and they are both younger than I, so they might succeed in taking my life. But I will not make it easy for them.

I returned to my guests with some food: flat breads, roasted eggplant, and cheese. They had apparently sensed that they had managed to grab my interest, and that I was unusually eager to hear what they had to say. They thus asked if they could start the story from the beginning, and I agreed. I was astonished by what I heard. They began, "After Jesus was born in Bethlehem in Judea, during the reign of King Herod, Magi from the East showed up in Jerusalem asking, 'Where is the king of the Jews who has been born? We have seen his star and have come to worship him...'" If this was mockery, it was unnecessarily elaborate. No, as strange as this turn of events was, it must be explained otherwise. Surely this meant that the child Joshua had survived, and that when he was older, his parents had told him the story of our visit. I interrupted to ask them about the name, and they confirmed that "Jesus" is the Greek form of the Jewish name Joshua. I resisted the temptation to interrupt them immediately with further questions, to ask about Joshua's parents, and his cousin John and his parents, and what became of them all. As they continued, some of my lingering questions were answered, while others remained with me, and of course many new questions now raced through my mind. I was shocked to learn that Herod Antipas, another of the sons of Herod the Great (as he had come to be known), had executed John (surely the John in their story must be the older boy I had met), and then the Romans did likewise with Joshua. It was odd to think that the two young boys had survived beyond childhood despite the danger we had placed them in, and yet when they had died later it was still due to our scheme. So much to think about, and much to regret. Perhaps if Parthia had remained in contact with one or both of them, we could have lent them our aid, and things might have unfolded differently, for them and for us.

The story my guests told me ended with the incredible claim that Joshua's tragic fate was not the end, that God had brought him back to life after his execution. They asked me to believe these things and become his follower. I told them that this was a lot to process, and that I needed time to think about what they had told me. This was the absolute truth. After they departed, I sat back down and remained transfixed, unable to move, my mind racing. Could it really be a coincidence that these men came here and completed this unfinished tale from my own life? Should I tell them my own version of the story and crush their faith? Would they even believe me if I told them what I know? Should I feign belief simply to find out more? If I did so it would provide opportunities to satisfy my own curiosity, if nothing else. But their growing network of contacts throughout the Roman Empire might also provide me with useful tidbits of information which I could pass on to my lord the king of Parthia.

These strangers have certainly given me much to think about. I hoped to change history, but only in the realm of politics. How could I have helped to start a new religion, much less one that I do not and would never adhere to? Even if I told the truth about my role in this, would anyone believe me? Will their story, mine, or both continue to be heard by future generations? Might the stories I grew up hearing about Zoroaster have come about in the same way? Or could some higher power have moved my lord the king of Parthia to initiate this mission and bring these things to pass? Perhaps all human beings are mere pawns in some celestial intrigue more complex and unfathomable than we ever know. After all, so few people in the whole world know about the machinations that led to my mission to Judaea all those years ago. Perhaps fewer still, or none at all, discern the plots and subterfuges that spirits benevolent and malign play out with us as their instruments.

I can think of only one thing to do that might help me make sense of all this. There is only one other person in the whole world that I can talk to about this. I learned some years ago that Melchior had met his end while on a mission. But last I heard Balthazar still lives. I will seek him out and tell him what these strangers have told me. I wonder what he will make of all this...

ABOUT THE AUTHOR

Dr. James F. McGrath is the Clarence L. Goodwin Chair in New Testament Language and Literature at Butler University in Indianapolis. He teaches courses on biblical studies as well as the intersection of religion and science fiction. His current research includes the latter topic as well as the historical figures of Jesus and John the Baptist. He has published science fiction short stories in *Touching the Face of the Cosmos* (edited by Paul Levinson and Michael Waltemathe) and in his own (mostly nonfiction) book *Theology and Science Fiction*.